BOURBON PENN

31

November 2023

Bourbon Penn Issue 31
November 2023

Copyright © 2023 by Cognitive Wave, Inc.

www.bourbonpenn.com
Myrtle Beach, SC

Editor:
Erik Secker

Copy Editing:
J. Scott Wilson

Cover Art:
On Va Fluncher
copyright © by arnus

Very special thanks to:
George Tom Elavathingal, Jen Lin,
Ioanna Papadopoulou, and Sam Rebelein

"Mesdames" copyright © 2023 by Naomi J. Williams
"The Louder I Call, the Faster It Runs" copyright © 2023 by E. Catherine Tobler
"An '80s Tenement Love Story" copyright © 2023 by Anthony Panegyres
"There Are Only Two Chairs, and the Skin is Draped Over the Other"
copyright © 2023 by Alexia Antoniou
"Tone Deaf" copyright © 2023 by Corey Farrenkopf
"The Right Time" copyright © 2023 by Nico Montoya
"Beach Day" copyright © 2023 by Shane Inman

CONTENTS

MESDAMES 7
Naomi J. Williams

**THE LOUDER I CALL,
THE FASTER IT RUNS** 39
E. Catherine Tobler

AN '80S TENEMENT LOVE STORY 61
Anthony Panegyres

**THERE ARE ONLY TWO CHAIRS, AND
THE SKIN IS DRAPED OVER THE OTHER** 91
Alexia Antoniou

TONE DEAF 105
Corey Farrenkopf

THE RIGHT TIME 125
Nico Montoya

BEACH DAY 143
Shane Inman

MESDAMES

——————— ■ ———————

Naomi J. Williams

Of course Anna said yes when they offered her the position. It meant the difference between destitution and a more restful old age for her mother. It meant all of her siblings going to school in shoes, with lunchboxes, until they graduated. It meant having her own room and bathroom. She might have said yes for that alone.

Strange rumors had swirled around the estate for years. Rumors always swirl around old families. But Anna hadn't seen anything untoward at the interview. Except their wealth, of course. Ancient carved lions at the front gate. Curving marble staircases outlined by mahogany banisters. Resplendent chandeliers hanging from coffered ceilings. Peacocks wandering the lawns. Peacocks!

The man who interviewed her never introduced himself. He might have been the man of the house, the family accountant, a steward, a butler—not that she knew the difference between the last two. They needed someone to replace a servant nearing retirement, he said. Anna would work with the older woman until she was ready to take over her duties.

"You need nerves of steel here," he said.

She told him that she took care of her mother and her siblings when they were sick, which was often.

"Steelier than that," he said.

She told him that she gutted the fish and skinned the rabbits her brothers brought home and wrung the necks of the chickens herself.

He stared back at her, impassive. So she told him that when her father was shot in the street she had tried to stanch the blood with her bare hands, then reached into his shattered chest to try to massage his heart back to life.

"That's what I mean," he said.

"That wasn't nerve," she told him. "That was love."

He handed her an envelope containing more money than she'd ever seen at one time. He showed her out through the rear entrance—"This is the door you'll use from now on," he said—and had a driver take her home to give the money to her mother and say her good-byes.

• • •

She did not live on the third floor with the other servants. A silent footman showed her to the second floor and delivered her to Ursula, the old servant she'd been hired to replace, a wide-hipped woman with a wiry gray braid down her back.

The tiny room in which Ursula installed her had originally been a closet. Her bed was a narrow monastic cot tucked under a narrower window, a window that let in a draft at night. Anna smiled to think that even in rich people's homes, windows leaked. But it was her own tiny room, attached to her own, even tinier, bathroom, and she was content for the present.

Ursula occupied a larger room across the hall. "It will be yours before long, if you prove yourself," she told Anna.

At first her only task was delivering meals. She would take the back stairs to the kitchen, where the head cook would pass her a lacquered tray arrayed with dainty dishes of dainty food. Anna would make her careful way upstairs, knock on the double oak doors across from her room and next to Ursula's, and hand the tray to Ursula, who always opened the door just wide enough to admit the tray. Thirty minutes later, Anna would knock again, retrieve the tray, and return it to the kitchen. Five times a day: breakfast, lunch, tea, dinner, and something called a *nightcap*, which turned out not to be a hat worn to bed but a drink, often served with a tiny saucer of nuts or chocolates.

The trays amused her, comprised exactly as one might imagine for consumption by the filthy rich: soft-boiled eggs perched on their own porcelain cups; tea steeping in flowery English teapots; demure squares of cucumber sandwich, crusts surgically removed, topped with parsley and arranged on gilt-edged plates; whole quail hiding under silver domes; jewel-toned drinks served in cordial glasses.

She wished she could regale her family with descriptions of these trays. She wished she could fling one down the marble staircase just to hear the music that metal, bone china, and crystal might make on cold stone.

"Good girl," Ursula told her once, receiving a tea tray. "You have steady hands."

It was true. But her care seemed pointless, for the person behind the double doors, the person Ursula attended to all day, broke things all the time. The lacquered tray was often handed back to Anna with a cracked teacup, two halves of a platter, forks with bent tines, or all the food smashed up together, as if an angry baby had been at it.

She knew it was no child. The delicate plates, the fussy meals, the food left uneaten: a woman lived behind the oak doors, a woman who could not or would not leave the room.

Between mealtimes, Anna wandered the unpeopled rooms and corridors of the great house. She liked the library, with its decadent aromas of leather and cigar smoke and passions trapped between book covers. Sometimes she ventured through the back door and explored the outbuildings and gardens and woods. Sometimes she sat in one of the unattended automobiles. The doors were always unlocked, keys left in the glove compartment.

No one ever stopped her. Not, she decided, because she was permitted free range over the estate but because no one dared speak to her. A village worth of people worked the place, footmen and chambermaids, gardeners and farmhands and mechanics—but they remained strangers. Eventually she began taking books from the library up to her closet. Eventually she figured out how to turn on the cars, then make them go and stop and turn and reverse. At dusk, when no one else was out, she'd take one for a spin around the property.

The only people she interacted with were Ursula, the cook, and occasionally, the man who'd hired her.

Early on he had accosted her and Ursula in the corridor and asked how things were going.

"She'll do, I think," Ursula said. "Incurious, which is good."

Anna tried not to smile.

"You don't have any questions?" the man said.

"Yes," she said. "Whose room is that?" She pointed to the double doors.

"It's the Mrs.'s, of course," Ursula said brusquely, as if Anna should have known.

Mrs.'s, Anna repeated in her head. *Missuses*.

And this, she thought, looking at the man, must be the *Mister*. He was not nearly as old as she'd thought at first. He had a full head of hair, curly and dark except for a bit of gray at the temples. Care more than time had aged him, she decided.

She grew impatient to assume her proper role in the house. Really she just wanted Ursula's room. It boasted an east-facing window, a small dining table where she and Ursula took silent meals together, a real bed, and a door that communicated directly with the unseen Mrs.'s room. But Ursula didn't seem eager to leave her position or her room. Now that she had someone to climb the stairs with the food trays, she appeared satisfied.

One night a commotion woke Anna from her cot under the drafty window. She rushed out to the corridor, fearing a fire. The double doors opposite were wide open, a steady wail issuing from the darkness within. Ursula stood in the doorway in a nightgown, her gray locks spilling out of an old-fashioned sleep bonnet. *Well,* there's *the nightcap,* Anna thought, but then another tall oak door opened down the corridor. The Mister emerged and ran toward them. He stopped when he noticed Anna, at which Ursula noticed her too.

"Back in your room," Ursula hissed. "You're not even dressed!"

"We might need her," the Mister said.

Ursula shook her head. "She's not ready." Grasping his arm, she drew him into the room and shut the heavy doors behind them.

Anna remained in the corridor as the wailing continued. She considered the way Ursula had grabbed the man of the house and pulled him into the room. She thought about the older woman judging her as unready. An hour passed before the doors finally opened again. By then the wailing had ceased. Only the Mister stepped out. He looked drawn and pale. Blood stained his shirt.

He jumped when she spoke, then stared through her thin nightgown. "Aren't you cold?"

She laughed. Even exhausted by emergency, a man will notice a woman's body. "Did she have a baby?" she asked.

"No," he said, "nothing like that."

"When am I taking over for Ursula?"

He regarded her with eyes too spent even to register pity. "Trust me," he said. "Whenever it happens, it will have been too soon."

A month later, when Ursula tripped in the corridor, she yowled with such vigor that even the chambermaids who avoided that wing came running. Anna reached her first.

"Get the doctor," Ursula ordered hoarsely.

"What doctor?" Anna said, kneeling beside her. "Will cook know who to call?"

"The doctor, you foolish child," Ursula said, then resumed yelling, which reverberated wonderfully over the hard surfaces of the corridor—slate floor, paneled walls, mosaic ceiling tiles, brass fixtures, tinkling glass.

Fortunately the Mister appeared.

"*This* doctor," Ursula panted.

Doctor? Anna had not realized that the Mister was a doctor.

Ursula was not a small woman, and even with two strong sets of arms, it was an effort to help her to her room. The Mister—*Doctor*, Anna would now think of him—sent her for ice.

When she returned, Ursula was saying, "It's the worst possible time for this."

"It can't be helped," the Doctor said.

After applying a compress to Ursula's swollen ankle, he brought Anna out into the corridor. "When you bring up the nightcap," he said, "knock on the door and come on through." He opened his mouth as if to say more but did not elaborate.

"Yes, sir," she said, then turned to sit with Ursula.

"Also," he said, "I found these in the corridor. Make sure there aren't any more." He reached out and dropped several cat's-eye marbles into her hand.

It was an imposing room, ornately appointed. In the dim light, she could make out the broad outlines of furnishings she couldn't yet name: armoire, divan, secretary desk, Persian rugs. And at the far end, behind a four-panel folding screen, a large canopied bed from which thrashing and stifled moans could be heard.

The Doctor sat glumly in a tall armchair. He gestured for Anna to set the tray on a side table, making no motion to bring the nightcap to his patient. He handed Anna a light blanket. It was the softest wool she had ever touched.

"Make yourself comfortable in a chair or on the floor," he said. "Sleep if you can. Don't come behind that screen unless I call for you."

She sat on the floor, leaning against the wall. How could she fall asleep while the Mrs. writhed and whimpered on the other side of the screen and the Doctor sat in the armchair, so near, listening for a crisis? The sounds frightened and stirred Anna, suggesting alike the torments of illness as well as the pleasures of the body. Yet when the Doctor did call her, sharply—"*Anna!*"—she jolted awake. It was near dawn, gray light leaking through heavy curtains. Scrambling to her feet, she passed behind the screen and approached the bed.

The stench assailed her first, a cloying perfume of sweat, blood, and excreta mixed with decay. It reminded Anna of the refuse heap outside her village, a rank place where they discarded everything from broken chairs to spoiled food to dead cats. The Mrs.'s large canopied bed looked like a battlefield, covers thrown every which way. A woman—the Mrs., it must have been—naked, pale, and far too thin, crouched at one end, glistening with sweat and crying out as she flailed and struggled against something on her back. Anna thought at first the woman was tangled up in her own sheets, but no, something larger and more substantial clung to her, something alive and feral and malign, something that had attacked the Mrs. and would not let go. Anna remembered the one time she'd seen a rabid dog. But how could a dangerous animal have made its way into the house, much less the room or the bed, while the Doctor kept watch?

The Doctor was on the other side of the bed, facing the Mrs. and wrestling against sinewy gray limbs. Anna could not tell in the darkness whose limbs they were or whether they were arms or legs.

"Keep it from biting her!" he shouted.

Anna stepped toward the bed, the tallest bed she had ever seen outside of a storybook, and prepared to climb on to the feather mattress to take hold of the furious creature entwining itself around the Mrs. But at her approach the creature turned its head and she saw its face, shrunken and spongy with decomposition but unmistakably human and female, its leaking eye sockets fixed on Anna as its mouth opened in a silent scream, skinny teeth parting across fetid strings of slime. The room grew suddenly cold and even darker; only the maw of the *thing* remained in sight, widening and widening till she fell in and drowned.

· · ·

When she came to, she was not in the Mrs.'s room. Or Ursula's room. Or her own closet. She tried to sit up, then fell back against a wave of dizziness.

"I told you: nerves of steel," the Doctor said. When she said nothing, he added, "Was it true, that story about trying to keep your father alive after he was shot?"

"What *was* that?" she said.

"The former Mrs."

Missuses, she remembered. "And where am I now?"

A pause. "This is my room." After a minute, he said, with some exasperation, "Ursula is right. You are strangely incurious."

"You should have told me."

He sighed. "We've found it makes little difference whether we warn people in advance or not."

"What did you do after I fainted?"

"I injected her with a sedative," he said heavily. "That settles them both. It's a last resort. Her heart is not strong."

Both. She found she could sit up a little. He brought her a glass of water. "So is that as bad as it gets?"

He barked a short, bitter laugh. "God, no. When her husband returns, it will be worse."

She could not hide her astonishment. "*Husband*? So *you* are not—?"

"*Me*?" He laughed again, with more mirth. Her face warmed. "No, no, no. I am not a family member." He snorted. "Thank God."

Later that day, insisting she was fine, Anna helped bathe the Mrs. The Doctor supervised from the doorway. Anna smiled to see the way he stood, primly turned away from his patient, as if he had not wrestled with her naked body a few hours earlier.

In the harsh light of the Mrs.'s opulent bathroom, the true atrocity of her situation was clear. She was young, only a few years older than herself, Anna guessed. She remained groggy from the drugs; if she were aware that a new person was bathing her, she didn't object. The desiccated body of her predecessor clung to her piggyback-style, its shriveled legs wrapped tightly around the Mrs.'s hips. More hideously, the flesh of the old wife's left hand was sunk into and melded with the flesh of the Mrs.'s left breast. The old wife emerged like an appalling growth from the Mrs.'s own body—or perhaps it was the other way round, the new Mrs. springing from the old. Anna thought suddenly of the women of her village, how they carried water and firewood and children on their backs, toiling under burdens they could not relinquish.

Anna drew warm water from the gold-plated faucet and poured it over the Mrs.'s embattled body and tangled black tresses. There was a raw bald spot at the back of her head. The old wife must have pulled or bitten out her hair. Anna wondered if the woman had ever been beautiful, and she wasn't sure if she meant the old wife or the new.

Delicate whirls of blood appeared in the bathwater.

"She's menstruating," Anna said.

"Yes," the Doctor said from the doorway. "That's when the worst attacks occur."

Anna did not cry till afterward. After helping the Mrs. out of the tub, after gently drying her off, even passing a towel over the spongy mass on her back, after dressing her in her specially-made clothes, arranging her in the armchair, and hiding the awful protuberances under scarves and veils. After the Mrs. turned weary brown eyes to Anna and whispered, "Thank you," a courtesy that broke her heart. Only then did Anna make her way through the double doors and sink to the hard floor of the corridor. Her hands began to shake and then her entire body.

"Drink this," the Doctor said, squatting beside her. He held a small glass to her lips with one hand and steadied the back of her head with the other. The remedy tasted at once bitter and sweet, cool and warming.

"Better?"

She shook her head and he proffered another sip.

"Are they—what is that called? Siamese twins?"

"No."

"How did it happen?"

"I don't know," he said. "I came afterward. I was brought—and bought—to stay here. Like you."

"They can't be separated?" she finally said.

"We've had specialists from around the world. Each attempt nearly killed her."

He emptied the glass himself and winced against its bittersweetness, but she could sense how it eased some tension in his body. She felt herself surrendering to a delicious sense of all-rightness.

"I made up the story about my father," she said, and nodded off to his laughter.

Ursula's ankle was slow to heal. But she relinquished her role with surprising alacrity, as if the sudden, forced cessation of her labors had brought her a relief she had forgotten she needed. Every day she sat propped up in a cushioned rocking-chair in her room and seemed to relish instructing Anna in the care of the Mrs. She said more in the week after her injury than she had in the previous three months.

For her part, Anna took pleasure in ignoring or upending Ursula's directions. The Mrs. hated the soft-boiled eggs that cook sent up every morning, so Anna changed the order to toast with jam. Then changed it to *two* slices of toast with jam, one of which she ate herself on her way upstairs each morning.

She also saw that Ursula's admonition to "never aggravate the old Mrs." was nonsense. The "old Mrs." was hostility incarnate—if "incarnate" could include rotting flesh. The free right arm, withered and usually limp, often came to furious life during meals, jerking suddenly, spilling hot tea on the Mrs. or jabbing her with a fork.

Sometimes Anna found these antics comical and had to stifle her laughter. But she sincerely pitied her mistress and started binding the errant arm to the chair back with a leather strap. The malicious creature then began squeezing its prey's left breast with its embedded hand until the Mrs. screamed in pain. At which Anna stabbed embroidery pins into the old arm until it stopped.

With food she preferred and fewer interruptions while she ate, the Mrs.'s appetite improved, and with it, her weight and color.

Anna also countermanded Ursula's injunction against saying anything about the outside world. "She cannot bear to hear it, poor thing," Ursula had said. But it wasn't true. When Anna brought in a newspaper she found in the library, the Mrs. asked her to please read it aloud to her, and sat rapt through every word, not just about the latest elections and wars, but notices of next week's flower show or the reunion of the class of whenever, as well as lurid reports of serial killers, freakish incidents, and faraway plagues.

"It's a dreadful story, Ma'am," Anna said, folding back a page of newsprint. She'd just read about a film shoot where a ghastly accident had decapitated the famous lead actor.

The Mrs. poured herself a second cup of tea. "I like to know I'm not the only strange thing in the world," she whispered. The Mrs. always whispered.

"Excuse my impertinence," Anna said after a moment, "but Ursula—was she lady's maid to the—the *first* Mrs.?"

The Mrs. looked up, and Anna could have sworn the shrouded head of the old Mrs. moved too. When the Mrs. nodded, so did the other head.

• • •

The man of the house returned. No one said where he had been or why. For all Anna knew, he might have been overseas—or simply in a different wing of the house. One day she opened the double door with the tea tray, and there he was, an old man, gray-headed but still vigorous, seated opposite his wife and talking far louder than necessary.

He was describing a fox hunt, of all things. Anna couldn't tell if it was a hunt he had participated in himself or had heard about. Some details about the horses and the drunken son of Lord Someone struck her as familiar. Perhaps he'd read about it in his own library. The Mrs. watched him politely but with nothing like the interest she'd shown in the newspaper. She fidgeted more than usual against her burden. The head of the old Mrs. held itself upright, at monstrous attention.

The man talked on and on, repeating himself—the dissolute son of the lord came up again, so drunk at ten in the morning he'd fallen off his horse, et cetera. The man was not really addressing the Mrs., Anna realized. Maybe he was talking to what was left of his first wife, who might remember some of the friends he mentioned. Maybe he was talking to himself, passing the time during an obligatory visit with his lawfully, awfully wedded wife. *Wives.*

"What have you done with old Ursula?" he suddenly asked.

"This is Anna, my dear," the Mrs. said. "She's been a great help."

"She's certainly better looking than Ursula," the man said with an unpleasant laugh. "That should help."

The Mrs. looked down, her face crimson.

"Are you all right, Ma'am?" Anna asked.

"Ursula needs to have a word with you," the Mrs. whispered without looking up.

"Is it true?" Anna demanded of the Doctor.

He blinked sleepily; she'd roused him from a nap, he claimed. "I'm sorry, Anna," he said. "It's a lot to ask—"

"No one's *asking*," Anna said. "I have no choice, do I?"

"I don't either," he said, closing his eyes. "We none of us do."

She wanted to cry, scream, stamp her feet. Instead, she drew in an unsteady breath and said, "I want more money for my family."

"We can do that."

"And a dose of that remedy of yours," she said. "I know you've been at it already."

• • •

The worst part was not leaning against the headboard with the spongy, rank creature pressed between her and the Mrs. and feeling it reanimate when the husband approached the bed.

It was not the ordeal of keeping the old wife from hurting the Mrs. during the encounter, an ordeal that showed up the next day in sore muscles and scratches and a bite that became infected.

It was not hearing the Mrs.'s shrieks as the old wife managed to claw or bite or pinch her anyway.

It was not the wretchedness of watching the old man working to contain his revulsion and outwit the languor of his own aged body.

It was not the effort required to keep from laughing, a laughter that threatened to turn into screaming if suppressed.

It was not seeing that, for all her torment, the Mrs. was roused by her husband's attentions yet found no release and was left panting and injured and bereft at the end.

It was not even the disgusting realization that the old man fixed his gaze on her, that it was Anna's face and body he was watching when he finally climaxed.

And it was not catching, over and over, the eyes of the Doctor as he struggled to keep the old wife's legs apart, to keep the creature from preventing the union of man and second wife, and exchanging in their glances a knowledge of their mutual degradation, a knowledge she found both mortifying and strangely provocative.

The worst part was Ursula, sitting in the armchair so she could ostensibly "coach" Anna, and the fevered avidity with which she consumed the tortured scene before her.

"I shouldn't give you any more," the Doctor said when she knocked on his door.

She knew then that he had just applied himself to the remedy, which she now knew came in brown glass bottles that he kept in a cabinet above his desk.

"That's not what I want."

"What *do* you want, Anna?" he said, his voice softer. A tiny ripple of hope surfaced over the exhaustion in his face.

"I want Ursula's room," she said. The ripple vanished.

Next day, Ursula was moved into the woodland cottage that had been readied for her retirement. Anna listened with satisfaction as the older woman's shouts of indignation and protest resounded in the corridor then down the back stairs then outside. She imagined the old woman being dragged away by her iron-gray braid. She could not stop smiling as she moved herself and her few belongings into the larger, east-facing room.

...

They started sharing breakfast, Anna and the Mrs., sitting as companionably at the table as a rich lady, her caretaker, and a malevolent appendage could manage. Anna had the newspaper delivered daily and read it aloud over their tea and toast. One morning she read that the local bishop had had to resign after allegations of molesting children in his diocese.

The Mrs. started to laugh.

Anna, for all her faithlessness, was shocked. "Ma'am?"

"That man came here to be feted in style, only to tell my husband he was a bigamist and I an adulteress unless we annulled our marriage," she hissed. "Now *he* is the outcast."

Anna had not considered the theological or legal ramifications of the Mrs.'s dilemma before.

"So you—are not legally married?"

"Oh, we are," the Mrs. said. "We eventually found a willing clergyman."

"I see," Anna said. What she saw most clearly was the way wealth allowed for contingencies of all kinds. "But how horrible for all those children."

"What children?"

"The ones attacked by the bishop."

"Oh yes, of course. Dreadful."

Anna wondered whether any of her siblings had wandered into this abhorrent man's orbit. She herself had rarely attended church, but her younger siblings sometimes went, as it pleased their mother.

That night, called upon to assist at the marital bed, Anna screwed up her face into such grotesque, unappealing expressions that the husband could not perform and eventually stormed off in naked rage, bellowing about how he was the most unfortunate man in the world.

The Doctor came to Anna's room after sedating the Mrs. and tending to her wounds. A visible pulse throbbed at his temple. Anna wished she could reach out and touch it.

"What were you playing at?" he demanded.

"Nothing." She looked away, fingertips tingling.

"I *saw* you, Anna. I had to stitch a laceration over her right eye. There are bites on her neck."

"I tried."

"You *tried*. What were those faces you were making?"

Her cheeks burned. "I hate the way he watches me."

He sighed. "I know, Anna."

"You do *not* know."

He brought a shaking hand to his brow, pressing at the angry temple. "You're right," he said. "But I do see how he looks at you, and I—"

"*Stop.*"

"I hate it too." He stretched an arm toward her as if to offer comfort.

She moved away. She still wanted to touch him; she wanted him to touch her. But not like this.

Inauspicious and terrible couplings notwithstanding, the Mrs. became pregnant. Anna was the first to know. The Mrs.'s sudden aversion to her nightcaps and chocolate was Anna's first clue. The second was breast tenderness so exquisite the Mrs. flinched from the pressure of her own clothes. When the month passed with no bleeding and no attack from the old wife, Anna told the Doctor. He blanched.

"Shouldn't we be happy?" she said. "Isn't this what it's all for, to produce an heir?"

"I didn't think it would ever happen," he said. "I don't want to imagine what comes next."

Her condition seemed somehow to have rendered the old Mrs. quiescent, but they did not speak aloud of the pregnancy in front of the mother-to-be, who came to her own understanding soon enough. They kept the husband away, anxious that his presence would rouse the old Mrs. to resentful comprehension. Instead the master and mistress of the house began writing notes to each other, which Anna, their courier, found charming in spite of herself: "My dear, I hope you are eating well, remember you now eat for two," "Dear love, Anna is having to let out my dresses again, I am growing quite round, you would not know me," and so on. Meanwhile the gray form of the old Mrs. hung limp behind her like a gruesome costume the new Mrs. had forgotten to take off.

"How is she?" Anna asked the Doctor one afternoon, after a somber-faced check on his patient.

He shrugged. He alone seemed unable to enjoy the lighter, more hopeful atmosphere in the house. If anything, he was more on edge than ever. He'd lost weight. It concerned Anna, although it also gave him a kind of consumptive beauty she rather liked.

"Maybe this will cure her," Anna said.

"Maybe."

"*Maybe,*" she said, imitating his dour tone.

His face flashed with ire, but he couldn't sustain his pique when he saw her smile. "Hope is very seductive," he said. "Have a care."

She could smell the sour aftertaste of the remedy on his breath. "It's a healthier seduction than others I could name," she said, then walked away before he could protest or misunderstand.

The Doctor was right to be wary, of course, although his anxiety, like most anxiety, proved worthless in the end.

Anna sensed the change one morning when she found the Mrs. restless and without appetite at breakfast. That would not be unusual late in pregnancy, but a faint corrosive smell hung about the room, a smell Anna recognized too late. When the Mrs. cried out and doubled over, Anna mistook it for a precipitous onset of labor, like in films, where the actress who never looks pregnant enough suddenly clutches at her stomach. Back in her village, Anna had never seen labor come on like this, and this is what she was thinking when she went to the Mrs.'s side and found that the long-dormant right arm of the old wife had awakened, crept up the side of the pregnant woman, discovered the swollen belly, and begun savagely clawing at it.

All of Anna's strength could not pry the arm away and she finally leaned over and bit it. The Mrs. screamed in pain, but the odious hand let go. Anna's mouth filled with a putrescence that made her gag. By the time she made her way down the corridor to waken the Doctor, the hideous arm had recovered and was attacking the Mrs. once more.

The Doctor staggered in, face gaunt, eyes unfocused, speech garbled. Anna wanted to slap him into wakefulness but instead ordered strong coffee brought up from the kitchen, an urn of it, please, and two cups, quick as can be. By then it was impossible to distinguish labor pangs from the old wife's abuses. Anna sent a note to the Mister. It told him what was happening and exhorted him to stay away, for the love of God.

He did not stay away. They never do, the men who need to stay away. He arrived in all his caviling mastery and stood, first, in the open doorway, then at the foot of the bed, refusing to leave, refusing to help, wildly bemoaning his fate. The Mrs. was bleeding—from the birth canal, from her nipples, from wounds inflicted by her tormentor. The husband would not hear of taking her to the hospital.

"She will die," the Doctor said.

"Just save the child," the Mister said. Then he resumed his lamentations: "Why, God? Oh, it is insupportable!" and all the rest.

Someone had informed Ursula as well, for here she was, supporting the Mister in her beefy arms as they stood weeping before the awful spectacle. Anna saw that, for all her cries of "My poor darling!," Ursula looked—not *happy*, no, that was impossible, but—fulfilled? Yes, perhaps that was the word. Anna didn't have the time or composure to consider what this meant, but later, when it was all over and she was far away, she would remember Ursula's expression that day and imagine, just for a moment, that she saw the truth of that terrible house.

Mercifully, it was over by sunset. The Doctor administered many times the normal dose of sedative and cut the baby out of the Mrs.'s body. Ursula wrapped the infant, a boy, in linens and left with the Mister. When the Doctor arranged the Mrs.'s body on the bed, the old wife slipped off of her like a shed snakeskin. Then two dead women lay in the bed. The Doctor, bloodied from head to foot, sank to the floor.

Anna took the key from the prostrate doctor's pocket and went to his room. She set aside one clean change of clothes, took a box heavy with cash, and stuffed as many of his belongings and medical instruments as she could fit into an old suitcase, emptying every brown bottle she discovered as she worked. She found seven. In her room, she set aside a change of clothes for herself, then stuffed into a satchel her own stash of money as well as a few books she had "borrowed." She carried the suitcase and satchel and box of money to the darkened library downstairs, which was near the back entrance. Then she tiptoed to the garage and, as quietly as she could, running lights off, drove the plainest, oldest automobile and parked it by the rear door.

Upstairs, she took the clean clothes back to the Mrs.'s bedroom. The Doctor remained on the floor below the bed. He looked at her glassy-eyed, and she searched him until she found another small vial of the remedy.

"One last time," she said, helping him drink the remaining drops.

He did not object when she stripped him of his bloody clothes and directed him into the Mrs.'s marble bathtub. He did not object when she stripped herself and joined him. He did not object when she rinsed the gore from their bodies or helped him out of the tub and into his clean clothes. He said nothing while she poured lamp oil over the bed and its occupants, finally at rest. He watched in silence as she lit the candles in the Mrs.'s silver candelabra. His eyes widened briefly when she threw it on the bed and the flames shot up. He did not look back as she led him from the infernal room, down the back stairs, out of the house, and into the car. He evinced no surprise when she started the engine and drove toward the gates of the estate. He groaned when she braked suddenly before the stone lions. She climbed out of the car to have a look.

She laughed as she resumed her seat. "I ran over a peacock."

He smiled languorously. He did not notice the red glow in the night sky behind them. He did not wake up when she stopped just before her old village to kiss her hand and lay it on the spot where her father had been shot. He slept beside her for hours as she drove, away from the glow in the sky, away from her village, away from the town where she had never gone to church, beyond anyplace she could have mapped. When they ran low on fuel, she stopped the car in an unfamiliar town, found lodgings that were cheap and asked no questions, managed to wrestle his drugged body out of the car and into bed, then crawled in next to him and fell asleep.

A few hours later she woke to find him looking at her with frank amazement. "Anna, where are we?"

"I'm not sure, but far."

"My things—"

She pointed to his suitcase on the floor. The sun was high in the sky, light leaking through rickety shutters, revealing the squalor of the room.

"My medical supplies?"

"As much as I could fit."

"Bless you," he said, climbing out of bed.

She listened as his rummaging grew more and more panicked. "I dumped them all out," she said.

"What?" He rose unsteadily to his feet.

"It's killing you."

She thought he was going to strike her, but when he saw her flinch, he uttered an anguished cry and sank to his knees beside the bed.

He was pale, sweating. "We have to go back."

"I set the place on fire."

"My God, I thought that was a dream."

She shook her head.

"Please, Anna, I need it."

"I know," she said. "But you need to not need it."

"You don't know what it's like," he said, his voice breaking. "The only thing worse than taking it is not taking it. I can't. I can't let you see me like that."

Her laugh was not kind. "You let me see a great many things, Doctor. Whatever happens next, it cannot possibly be worse."

He tried to smile. "Nerves of steel," he muttered between shallow breaths.

"No, you idiot," she said. "I told you before that that's not it at all."

She did not know whether he could recover, or, once better, stay recovered. She did not know whether they were being hunted, and if so, where they could be safe. She did not know what they would do when they ran out of money, although that would not be soon. She did not know whether they could love each other away from the estate, away from the Mrs., away from the horrors they'd endured together. But seeing the pain gather in his face, knowing that soon he would be terribly sick, she clambered out of bed and drew the ragged curtains across the windows to keep out the light for a little longer.

■

Naomi J. Williams is the author of the novel Landfalls *(FSG, 2015), long-listed for the Center for Fiction First Novel Prize. Her short fiction and essays have recently appeared or are forthcoming in* Electric Literature, Pangyrus, the Brevity Blog, LitHub, *and the* Future Fables *podcast. "Mesdames" is part of a collection of stories inspired by eerie Japanese tales. A biracial Japanese-American, Naomi was born and partly raised in Japan; she currently lives in Sacramento, California, and teaches with the low-res MFA program at Ashland University in Ohio.*

THE LOUDER I CALL, THE FASTER IT RUNS

■

E. Catherine Tobler

In the predawn dark, Annie found herself in a bed, holding onto another hand beneath the cool weight of the pillow. Floral case, it was the trailer—her trailer—and slowly she came back to herself, to her body, and kissed the folded fingers beneath the pillow before claiming the ringing phone, dreadful thing. The voice on the other end was frantic, offering double pay because the cops needed her—needed her boat, a man had gone missing—Ricky had that charter, didn't she remember—it had to be her, there was no one else. Triple, she said. She lived plain, but there were always bills.

She dressed in the dark, phantom chill of the lake already clinging to her. Her skin pebbled everywhere and she was surprised when she pulled her hair back into its customary tail that it did not leak lake water across her shoulders.

It was twenty-four minutes from the RV park to the lake, not counting the time she spent hitching the boat trailer to the truck. Years ago they'd told her: don't stay hitched overnight, anyone could drive away with the whole shebang. She'd never seen it happen, but there was plenty she hadn't borne witness to that still was in the record of the world.

The sun stayed hidden the whole way there. The roads were barren and she liked them that way, listening to the even breath of tires over asphalt. Dry, smooth. The trailer had a wobble, a squeak, but it would wait until the afternoon—depending how long they kept her out. A man had gone missing.

It wasn't the first time and surely wouldn't be the last. She had helped the law before—it was a fine diversion, given how well she knew the lake, its surrounds. Usually people wanted to know where the fish were: rainbow trout, sockeye salmon. A man was many times larger than a fish, but the lake was larger still. Sometimes the lake won.

The police were gathered near the boat launch when she arrived. One of them thought he could guide her with a set of flashlights, like he was bringing in an aircraft; she said nothing, backing her trailer into the water and paying him no never mind. Men—policemen—meant well on the surface, but it was easy to slip below.

She met each one and shook each's hand, and no one asked her name. They were all the same: overly warm in the cool morning air, redolent with musk and salt. Would be nice, one said, to get this done ahead of sunrise. The lake would be open then—it didn't need saying. Summer profits were on the line, no one needed a missing tourist mucking up a perfectly good summer day on the lake. Whistling lines and reels, cold beers, shining ice to cradle any legal catch.

The lake would win that battle, though; she didn't have to tell them it was five hundred feet at its deepest. If their man was in there, it could take a while. She knew the currents—where might a body go, they asked her. Wherever the lake liked, she said. You make it sound alive, one of them said with a cigarette-rough laugh, and she didn't reply, because the idea that the lake wasn't a living creature as any of them was absurd.

They went slower than any of the men liked; the radar on board wasn't the best, needed an upgrade, but the men waved it off during conversation; she was the real radar, knowing the lake like no one else did. She'd worked it so long now—how old, the youngest asked with a gleam in his hazel eye, and she said softly fifty, because it was a good number, given how old he thought she was. Just a grandmother to him, silver hair tied back to show every line upon her face. When the sun began to rise, she somehow looked younger, like a girl the youngest wouldn't hesitate to ask out, a stroll along the lakeshore where no one could go missing.

The radar sweeps showed fish and more fish; twice, the youngest shouted excitement over a fallen log, but the third time he wised up and let it pass in silence. The one in charge radioed the shore; told them the lake was closed until further notice.

She supposed they had good cause to believe this man was in the lake, but asked about other leads. There were two other lakes—but that this was the only natural one hadn't escaped her notice. The man-made lakes were tamer. The men hemmed and hawed; she went back to driving the boat. It was what she did; it was what she knew.

Steve Miller, they said, was a father. Wouldn't just wander off and leave his family to wonder. Plenty of things weirder than that had happened in the world, but she didn't argue. When her radio chirped with a call from Ricky, she also didn't argue with him, but told him in the covert way she had before to keep his eyes open. He was on the largest of the three lakes that day; maybe he'd turn up a missing father who'd never leave his family to wonder.

They came back to the launch for lunch. A crowd had formed behind yellow police tape some ways up the road. The police headed toward the lodge, but she stayed with the boat, not liking to eat with an audience. Eileen, who had called her that morning, waved from the porch of the lodge.

They didn't find Steve Miller that afternoon; the chief called it, on account of how many men he was paying to look. He didn't say it that way, but she heard it underneath it all. The chief asked her to come back tomorrow (he was bringing half his men); she said triple, and he bit down on the toothpick that had been working his teeth all afternoon. He didn't say no, just gave her a curt nod and headed out.

The lake remained closed. She didn't drive home, but lingered at the lodge, listening to the people speculate. It's what people did best, spinning tales about affairs, thefts, lake monsters. From the lodge's height, the lake didn't look so monstrous, flat blue and empty under the cloudless sky. It was the perfect postcard photograph, framed by quaking aspens that circled the lodge porch.

Eileen brought her usual salty Lambrusco spritz with its olives, and asked her about the lake, about being out there with the police. Eileen always wanted a salacious story, but there wasn't one here, not yet. The chief, she said, was cash-strapped, but that news didn't surprise Eileen, who moved toward the lodge doors at the arrival of more local reporters.

Men wandered off; it was the easiest explanation. They got into their own heads so deep about life and the universe, they just dropped off the face of the earth—sometimes for a few weeks, sometimes forever, heads finding new pillows on which to sleep. Even family men.

She chewed green olives and pondered the lake, watching the empty water. Not empty, of course—running with life where they could not see. The fish and the reeds and the worms and the frogs and the dragonflies. The mosquitos, the water hyacinths, the long grasses she had not learned the names of. She craved the lake water in her mouth and needed for the day to end, so that she could accomplish that without anyone's supervision.

But Eileen kept the lodge open late—people were worried, wanted to mingle and speculate because there was safety in numbers, and what if the man reappeared? The lodge lights would welcome him. Trusting the lodge lights would also mask the night-dark lake from view, she left the lodge as quietly as she had come. Truck and boat were where she'd left them, and she let them sit, hiking to the lake via no discernible path whatsoever. The water called her.

It was ritual, but it was also life, the way she answered the water's call. At the lakeshore, she stripped out of hoodie, sneakers, and jeans. Underwear came last, all of it left in a heap in the summer-cool grasses she did not know the name of.

She walked into the water until the bottom came out from under her, then she sank and swam. She should have perhaps been blind in the dark water, but she was not. Every sense came alive in the lake in ways they did not on land.

Beneath the water she could search in ways that she could not above. She took mouthfuls of the fresh water into her nose and mouth, veils of bubbles gathering at her temple, her collarbone, her hips. She strained the water between teeth and tongue, and spat out what was of no use. She pushed deeper into the lake, and deeper still, finding the point where freshwater was occluded by salt. Where blood stained the water, she knew.

He still looked human, but even another twelve hours could change that. His eyes were open, but he saw nothing of his surroundings. He was dressed in a suit, his tie tangled around a log, holding what remained of him in place. To her relief, he possessed both hands, but his spine gleamed like pearl beyond where a monstrous mouth had taken most of his left side. The liver, she thought, the fatty, delicious liver.

Morning brought rain. The chief wore a plastic cap over his official hat, a camo rain poncho over his uniformed shoulders. He brought only two men with him this time, each also wrapped in plastic.

She took them out as she had yesterday, listening to them speculate about the man they sought. A real dirtbag, one offered up; Steve Miller looked like a family man, but harbored secrets the same way the lake did. In the wrong place at the wrong time, said the other; Steve Miller was a family man, but saw a thing he shouldn't have seen. Were others out looking elsewhere, she asked, and was given a sharp scowl for an answer. She wasn't in a hurry, given she was occupied with silent speculation all her own.

The lake had been her home—her world—for a while now. She would have to sit down and work out the years, because years meant something different to her than they did to these men. She could say she remembered the price of fuel for her boat had once been .50 cents, and was now $3.11, but that didn't tell her how much time had passed.

No matter how long she'd been here, she had been careful. What she required to live, the town and its surroundings gave her. She had never taken more than was necessary. There had been other deaths throughout the years of course, but this was unlike those—this was something akin to *her*.

It made her uneasy. She hadn't slept for the way the idea kept her thinking long into the night. There wasn't supposed to be another like her here—they kept their distances intentionally, so they could pass unseen, so they could live. Matings happened, offspring came, but they were taught solitary lives, so that no person would know the truth beneath their skins. It could have been a youngling, she thought, especially given how careless it all was. Someone known, a family man—she would never.

When the police began to grumble at her seeming ineptitude, she gave them another half hour of it, then maneuvered the boat closer to the submerged body. She drove slower and scanned more carefully; a school of fish fled the crime scene, darts shooting north.

Looks promising, she said, and showed them the logs and debris on the radar, all places where things might get stuck. Things like bodies, one man asked, and she gave no answer; he didn't want one. She slowed so the men could drop their underwater camera rig into the lake. The chief gave over controls to one of his men, seeming confused by the tech, or the responsibility that arrived with the body's discovery.

The monitor showed what she had seen last night, the logs and the trapped body. But the man was floating upside down now, more of the body missing. The sight sent a chill through her; the predator had returned?

The chief let out a hard breath when he saw the body; said it looked like a shark had been at it. She couldn't help but agree, even though they knew sharks didn't live in these waters.

The chief had enough speculation for the both of them; she cut the engine and dropped anchor while he blathered on. He called for the coroner to come out, which took long enough the men were verbally dreaming about lunch. The chief wondered how they could think about food at a time like this, but his own growling stomach gave him away.

The men paced the length of her boat as they waited for the coroner's team; the youngest smoked, even though he was asked not to. She didn't mind, thought it made him smell more interesting. Younglings were interesting, after all, for the way they didn't conform. The more she considered the body, the more she grew fixed on the idea that what had killed Steve Miller was young.

It wouldn't be a police matter, she thought as the coroner's boat arrived. The police would try—she had seen it before—but they wouldn't understand what they were looking at. In these mountains, it would probably be chalked up to a bear. It made the most sense, and most people wouldn't read the details—what was a bear doing in the lake, at that depth? Bears didn't feed like that, or hunt like that, even in desperation. But people didn't care; tell them a bear had killed a man, that was all they'd hear.

A bear wouldn't necessitate the closure of the lake; they would call the rangers, see what they might find—a mother wandering with her new cubs—and would work to relocate the offender. That would be that, unless the presumed youngling wasn't set on a new course.

She chewed the inside of her cheek until she tasted blood. That wouldn't be that unless she found the truth of the death. No bear, but her own kind, and she had never—

Couldn't fathom how, but when the body came up, pale and bloated like something from another time altogether, she knew one way. The youngling had come back, perhaps thought its cache of meat was safe. The youngling *would* come back.

Camera shutters, calculations, conversations had by small huddles of smaller men. She had nothing to do but watch the men work. Two divers went down, bringing up things that had likely been in the man's suit pockets. A key for the lodge, a wallet, a wad of sodden paper.

The team spread these things upon a shaky folding table and photographed them one by one. She leaned in to see the wallet, spread open to show the drivers' license—to show this man was not Steve Miller, but someone else entirely. Wallace Crescent, from Oak Park, Illinois.

The chief bit out a curse and she leaned against the rail, looking into the waters. They moved slowly, reflecting the day's gray sky between lazy raindrops. Another body meant Steve Miller was still out there somewhere and maybe the youngling wouldn't come back.

When the chief felt the scene was secure, he sent the coroner on his way, and then turned to her at the rail. The chief wanted another sweep of the lake, as many as it took, to ascertain they hadn't missed their target. His eyes were unsettled; he had a considerable problem on his hands now and knew it.

She raised the anchor and they set back out, scanning, always scanning. The youngest officer stood beside her, asking where they were on the map. She pointed, showed him where the body had been, and he made marks on the lake map, checking off sections as they scanned through them. Sunken logs, tumbled boulders, the prow of another boat, a rack of mossy antlers looking like a melting candelabra as it peeked out of the lake. The moose she had taken a summer ago, she thought, but didn't see the skeleton as they passed by. A moose, the young officer guessed, and she nodded, idly.

He marked it on the map with a big M, and they continued on, no sign of their family man emerging from the lake by the time the chief's patience had worn through. At the boat launch, she kept out of his way, taking the warm Thermos Eileen offered her. It was filled with salty homemade chicken soup.

The chief ordered the lake closed one more day, but said he wouldn't need her services. She watched him walk away with his men, and radioed Ricky from her truck. Ricky hadn't turned up a blessed thing, and when she told him they'd found the wrong body, there was a strange pleasure in the whoop of laughter she heard over the channel. She supposed Ricky and Eileen were the closest she had to friends; their reactions provoked something similar in her.

For a second night, she didn't drive home. She sat in her truck and felt something she hadn't felt in a long while: utter confusion over what to do. She'd lived here long enough that the days had their own rhythm. Nothing untoward happened here. She lived off the land the way countless other animals did, and one path never interfered with another. One life kept clear of the other. Until now.

Beyond her windshield, the world darkened. Crickets made themselves known, but fireflies rarely roamed this far north so the woods remained unspangled. Only the sky put on its starry show and she watched the distant, dead light, pondering the potential youngling.

It wouldn't be unheard of—had surely happened before somewhere. In every culture, younglings went off, thinking they knew what they were about, believing they understood the world they inhabited. A wrong step didn't scare them because they believed themselves unbreakable if not immortal. Wounds would heal, so why not leap off every cliff presented to them?

She found the youngling on the lakeshore where she'd gone in the water the night before. It was no bear, but her own kind. Young, male, it added up. Males often got it into their heads more than females that they couldn't die or be killed. She thought it was the process of giving birth that did it—carrying another life, birthing it. The experience changed a body, a mind, enough to know how haphazardly life was bound into a physical shell. The slightest mishap could send it fleeing.

The youngling was naked and crouched on all fours, smelling the grass where she'd discarded her clothes. She watched him in silence as he took a mouthful of grass and chewed the taste of her out of it. Piss would have been more effective, but she hadn't had to mark territory since coming here.

Maybe he caught her scent when the wind shifted, maybe the long line of her shadow edged into the corner of his vision. Either way, he jumped backward at the discovery of her, feet sliding down the gentle bank and into the water; in his panic he vomited the grass he'd eaten, and pedaled backward into the lake.

She moved swiftly, pursuing him into the water. He made no sound but for the splash of water, mouth seemingly sealed against complaint. He dropped beneath the surface and she followed, lunging to take hold of his arms. He felt human, he looked human—they all did—but she knew he was not. As he knew she was something other, so she knew of him.

He also knew he wanted to get away—seemed to instinctively know that she understood his transgressions and had come to settle the matter with him. This territory was not his—he knew it wholly, the way one understands an arm is his own—and further, worse, mistakes had been made. Men had been taken.

She was old and perhaps wise, but he carried with him the luck of youth, the strength—the ability to surprise. She was solid, but he wedged an elbow into her again and again, and slipped from her hold in an explosion of bubbles and mud, and when she could at last clear her eyes, he had gone. She pulled herself from the water and onto the bank where the scent of him lingered, and she vomited water until she was empty. Shock rushed through her—that he was here at all—and she could not think what to do, and so she left. Got back to her boat and her truck and left, until she'd circled back to the RV park. She walked through the pulsing waves of crimson neon. NO VACANCY it flashed, and she wished the youngling understood the meaning.

That he had chased her from *her* lake was not lost upon her. In the trailer, she showered the muck from her body then lay on the cool floral sheets. She sought the hand beneath her pillow. It looked so small now, withered in death; the man whose hand it had been had not been small. She had taken her time with him and wouldn't need another meal for some time, but the youngling ... He wouldn't understand the need for care.

She counted the ways on the hand before her—the ways she might help—and the idea of leaving was strongly at the top of her final list. Leave the lake to the youngling, go somewhere new, some place where she would not be noticed. But it was her lake—and she snarled at the idea of leaving it. The youngling would destroy the balance, would be found and—studied. She went cold at the word.

She studied the hand in her grip. It might have been Steve Miller—while she had destroyed the man's wallet, after extracting $12.76, she had not read his identification. She could recall no photographs, no anything to tie him to the missing Steve Miller. If it was Steve Miller, the police would never find him, deep in her belly.

She drove to the launch come morning, and there was Eileen with the chief. Arguing, she thought, and when Eileen slapped the chief, it was everyone in the vicinity who jerked in response. When she got to Eileen's side, the woman turned on her heel and vanished into the lodge.

Women, the chief muttered, then looked at the one who remained beside him. He made no apology, only lit a cigarette and took a long drag. He reminded her he didn't need her, that they'd cleared the lake, then he strode away, toward his men. She followed Eileen, taking a seat at the counter inside where the woman was crying.

"Sam's gone," Eileen sputtered. "Chief won't do a damn thing—says it's too soon and you know young men," she continued, imitating the chief, "they wander off, get drunk, and forget to call their mommas."

But Sam didn't, she thought. Sam was the responsible kind of offspring, helping his mother at every turn. He wanted to run the lodge someday. She gently touched Eileen's shaking hand, thinking about mothers and sons and how the youngling might've been taking other men down because he saw them as competition. There might have been no reason—she knew that too, because animals were animals and sometimes hunger had no source, only *was*—but she wanted a reason, if only to explain to Eileen, her human friend.

The lake would open in the morning, but for one more night it was hers. As she had before, she sought the water's edge, but crouched, listening, until long after sunset. The frogs began to sing, and deep in the trees the cicadas began, but when she opened her mouth to join, every other creature went silent. The sound that came from her was ancient, the kind of call scientists could only dream about knowing. It came from deep inside her, from a nameless organ—for her kind had never been discovered, dissected.

Her call rose from her body like a geyser, a building rush and then an exhale. A sound of isolation, of seeking. She had not called to others of her kind for longer than she could remember, and she did not want to do it now. She closed her eyes and called and called. Birds took nervous flight from nearby trees. The rest of the world did not move, did not breathe. Somewhere, she pictured a child sitting up in bed.

Dad, did you hear—what was it?

I don't know, honey—listen again.

She sank beneath the cool, dark water and opened her mouth to call again. The water changed the call—or the call changed the water, vibrations moving in every direction all at once. She became a focal point, the center from which all flowed—an antenna, tuning. *Come,* she said, *I am made ready.*

The youngling came because he was helpless to do otherwise. Her body was old, but she might mate yet again, and she gave every indication to the youngling that it was time. He approached her with mouth open, dragging in the scent of her. He leaned into her shoulder to smell her more deeply and that was when she smelled Sam on him. Eileen's offspring. Dead?

Her scent changed—from willing rut partner to hunter. She cursed herself as the youngling thrashed backward. She saw then the blood on him, the blood that had been trailed behind him. Human, crimson to her eyes even in the dark. The youngling fled. She followed.

He was not physically wounded, she thought, but something wasn't right—he'd been too long alone, had forgotten the ways of their world. He was still a cunning prey, eluding her easily because the scent of human blood masked him. She called to him again, but the lake grew still. The frogs and insects came back to their songs and she listened in defeat. Barefooted, she padded toward the blood trail, bent down and tasted it along with the dirt of the world. The world was old, the blood was new, and in this way she found him, Sam huddled inside a cave the youngling had been using. Sam startled at the sight of her, naked and smeared with mud, blood. He would know her as his mother's friend, but everything else about her would be unfamiliar. She stood unbowed before him. It was her lake.

"Your mother is at the lodge," she said.

"You're—" Sam broke off, shuddering.

What word would he have even chosen?

"Working," she said, and waited until he had gone before she searched the cave. Bones, scraps of fabric, nothing that made a life, only a layover. She rubbed her hands across the cave walls and pissed a line in the dirt before she left. Outside, under the clear summer sky, she lifted her voice in song once more. It was her lake.

The frogs went silent and the insects, too. In the near distance she heard him, panting and compelled to run toward her omnipresent call. He came faster and faster, on two feet and then four. At the sight of her he stumbled and fled anew. She followed after. There was an unhinged joy in the pursuit; the faster he ran, the louder she called. His knees buckled, body betrayed by instinct, and she rolled him into the long grasses she did not know the name of. His eyes would not focus and fever had made his skin clammy. His neck became fragile between her hands, his body easily limp, pinned beneath a log.

A bear, the papers said in the morning; the animal had been caught, tagged, and relocated. The lake flooded with tourists, with summer money. The chief assured everyone there was no cause to worry because bear attacks were rare, but here were the precautions they could take if they were concerned. Sam and Eileen stood nearby the chief, proof that the police had got their monster.

In the night, when the summer people had bedded down in lodge or boat, Annie lifted her voice to call once more and no bear came answering.

■

E. Catherine Tobler's short fiction has appeared in Clarkesworld, F&SF, Beneath Ceaseless Skies, Apex Magazine, *and others. Her novella,* The Necessity of Stars, *was a finalist for the Nebula, Utopia, and Sturgeon Awards. She currently edits* The Deadlands.

AN '80S TENEMENT LOVE STORY

∎

Anthony Panegyres

I don't own a dog. In the past we've kept the more disposable type of pet: goldfish, hermit crabs and meal worms. Hard to form an attachment with meal worms, isn't it? "It's all we can manage with our lifestyle," Dad always tells me. I'm pretty sure he's eaten a worm or two when I wasn't watching. He has that guilty look sometimes.

So, this dog I'm now following through the reedy marshes of the riverbank isn't mine. Sun's about to set, which means Dad will be home. You see, for a millisecond, when the sun sinks below the horizon, Dad flashes green. Snooze and you'll miss it, not be super aware and you'll miss it too.

At sunset, Dad's Law is for me to either be at home or completely isolated elsewhere—as I am now. Nobody comes into the marshes. Not with the mud and spiky stalks, and horseflies, swamp-flies and mossies, and let's not forget the tiger snakes. But this mongrel hangs out here. I'm visiting his home and escaping my own.

People around here call *mongrels* "mixers" or "bitsers." "*Mongrel* sounds rotten," they say, and the poetic ones add, "Think of the connotations." But I've no problem with the word.

I'd take a mongrel any day of the week over a genetically flawed pure bred; and this one's cute, like a miniature dingo (the bits that aren't covered in muck). White-tipped tail is the "crème de resistance," an apt phrase, as I've read that it's an ignorant conflation of "creme de la crème" and "piece de resistance": a *mongrelized* phrase.

He rolls over as soon as I see him. Might be a submissive gesture; may mean he's been mistreated before. I wonder whether the previous owners belted the loveable mutt and he ran away.

There's no collar. I haven't found a name for him yet. Sure, he's got a few ticks and fleas, and smells like marsh—all sulphurous eggs—but I don't care. My soles sink into the oozing muck as I dig my nails in and scratch the little guy all over his tummy and chest. His tail wags with endless energy.

AN '80S TENEMENT LOVE STORY

• • •

"Okay, Andrew," Dad says, while we're parked in our rusted metal box. "We'll run through it one last time."

"It's fine, dad. I only need to say the truth. How we're poor as shit."

Dad pinches my earlobe and twists. "No joking, Andrew. This could be big for us. Where's your mum?"

I whack his arm away. "Mum died. Six months ago." I don't actually have a mum. I mean I realize I must have somewhere along the line. But I never actually knew her. "Cancer," I continue, "ate her away until mum wasn't even there anymore. You left your job to take care of her. Didn't feel comfortable otherwise. Drained the finances. Lost the home. That's why we live in the crappy flat."

"Great—but don't say 'crappy'."

"And it was all worth it. Who needs money or a house when there's love?" Even though I'm fifteen, I say the last line like a pauper child begging for a morsel in *Oliver!* or some other Victorian era-based film.

Dad tousles my hair. I palm it back into place. "You're the best, kiddo. Nail it every bloody time."

You'd never guess my father is a goblin. I say "father" but I'm sure I'm adopted. Father disguises himself as a genuine salt-of-the-earth bloke, jeans and untucked shirt type of guy. Victims don't work out my father's a goblin until it's too late. They ignore his slightly pointed ears; his longer canines. The victim's relatives almost pick up on it: "You're not human", "What type of person does that?" "How do you live with yourself?" The raw emotional—and often physical—barrage continues until we abscond to another town or city.

We exit the car to find Aunty Rose waiting for us outside the gates of her swanky Mosman Park home, which is perched on a hill with river views. She's sprightly for a lady with a walking-frame. Probably should be in a home. We've been taking out "aunty" for lunch three to four times a week ever since our arrival in the neighbourhood—although she shouts[1] as much as us. Dad says our love and tenderness has led to a change in the will. "Locked-in like concrete. Only thing we can do wrong is fuck it up." We've been greasing those arteries of hers something chronic. Chicken nuggets, fries, chips, battered fish, Kentucky Fried Chicken, and when she's after a change—we get the equivalent grease-up from elsewhere, usually Asian.

Aunt Rose, who wheels over to the car on her frame, is pretty cool. I resist pinching my nostrils, her perfume is

---

[1] Shout: Australian for pay for another person.

intense and usually veils reality, but an odor still escapes at times, that's incontinence for you. Dad insists that he "can't smell shit" and laughs at his own joke.

I leap out of the car and help her into the front seat. Once in, I kiss her cheek. "Love your dress today, Aunty! Floral suits you." I put her walking frame in the boot then take a back seat.

"How's that girlfriend of yours?" she asks. "Kissed her yet? What's her name again?"

"Nadine. Thinking of holding her hand when we next go for a walk."

Whadoyouthink? We pash whenever we can. Nice to know Aunt Rose cares though. I'm nuts about Nadine. Think it's love. Kind of hope that Aunt Rose doesn't cark-it soon. Means being on the run again. Means no Nadine.

"What'll it be today, Rose?" asks Dad. "How 'bout something exotic? Chinese?'"

Over the last year, we've been living in some Mosman Park flats near the railway. Dad calls them "tenement Hellholes". He blows whatever we have with goblinesque stupidity. Goblins aren't renowned for their financial savvy; they're not stupid, just stupid with cash. In all other areas Dad's as cunning as a goblin.

Perth is a beautiful place, mirrorlike sheen of the river and a golden coastline, and we're smack-bang in-between them both. Palatial homes are on either side of our no-hoper area of flats. Our own flat is on the twelfth floor, with weirdos for neighbors on both sides. Dad has a habit of banging on the wall to no reply as one neighbor plays *Star Wars* repeatedly at eardrum-bursting decibels. I can't wait until *Empire Strikes Back* is released to video for a change in dialogue. On the rare moments the guy leaves his room, he has this whiff of porcine sweat. He looks like the Egyptian dude in *Raiders of the Lost Ark*. One day I'm going to ask him to bellow: "Indi! Indi! Indi!"

And on the other side is a guy I try to avoid at all costs. All Speed. And I don't mean the motocross. He's always on the point of explosion, and I don't want my head in the way of his fist when it transpires.

Aunty, dad, and I end up in the local Chinese restaurant. My role requires a fine equilibrium: I pepper the conversation with mum-lines and the rehearsed car routine: "I miss her so much you know", "Barely recognised her at the end," but I also have to keep the convo warm and jovial so we're good company for her. We serve up Aunty Rose an array of golden goodies. Golden deep-fried boxing wings, crispy golden deep-fried prawn parcels, deep-fried golden crispy chicken, crispy golden pork belly. Where does she put it all?

"Should we treat ourselves to dessert, Aunty?" says Dad.

I'm feeling queasy myself. Never thought I'd admit it, but I'm longing for green food, longing to degrease my mouth.

"Want some, Andrew?" she asks me. And right then the guilt hits me like a Michael Holding bouncer[2]. How on earth can we hurt this kind old bag?

"Pretty full myself."

"Look at him, Aunt Rose," says Dad. "Too polite. All skin and bones ain't he? Little dessert didn't hurt anybody. Sure, you've got room for golden fried ice cream!"

I shake my head, and the goblin's shoe cracks me in the shin.

He calls over the waiter. "Fried ice creams, please."

Aunt Rose smiles as she eats. "Never had this as a child; banana split was a big deal, or pavlova or cheesecake, but not fried ice cream." She dabs her lips with a trembling hand, then reaches into her purse. "For you, Andrew," she says, pulling out a twenty-dollar note. "Treat Nadine to a movie tonight. Buy her some popcorn, too."

---

[2] West Indies pace bowler. Bouncer: Dangerously high cricket ball to batsmen.

· · ·

We drop Aunty Rose off and arrange for another outing in a few days' time. She winks at me after I kiss her goodbye, and whispers in my ear, "It's for you." Not sure what she means, but I sense it's kind. By the time I think of saying something back, she's wheeled off on her frame.

In the passageway to our room, the Darth Vader theme booms out of the swine-scented nerd's door. Dad thumps a couple of times on his door before putting the key in ours.

"Okay, if I see Nadine?'"

"No problem," says Dad. "You did great today, apart from that crap with dessert. Be back before sunset."

"But that's at seven."

He grabs my shirt and pulls me close so all I can smell is his batter-riddled breath. "Be back before sunset." He releases me. "Go on, have some fun before then."

On the stairs down to Nadine's floor, I think of how Nadine had told me that her mum: "is good on her Good Days." I'd nodded and tried to give off an understanding vibe, so if she were comfortable, she could tell me more there and then, or, if too soon, she could open up later. One of those moments when you have to balance prying and consoling.

I wasn't sure if I'd got the ledger right.

But as I turn from the steps leading to her floor, guess who's in the passageway? Nadine wears a Star Trek T-shirt—she beats me in the geek states. She hurries toward me finger over her lips, and rushes past me. Over the back of her shoulder, she gives me the "come-on" signal. I follow her up the stairs all the way back to the floor I live on. She slumps against a passage wall. I hope my raised eyebrow looks cool and caring rather than just dorky. It's not the most romantic place: the carpet has a mildew odor and there are black pieces of old gum throughout, and whoever takes care of these communal spaces tends to miss cigarette butts.

"Not a Good Day," Nadine says.

I touch her arm to show I care, and she pushes it away.

"No offense," she says. "Not into the whole heal-the-victim-knight-in-armor thing. Give me a second and I'll be right." I back off, providing her space. She times her breathing, in and out, slowly, lids closed for half a minute, until she speaks: "Okay, I'm good. And now, so that you don't think you're taking care of me, *I'm* going to hug *you.*"

And she does. I hope I won't get an awkward stiffy like I did two days ago. Nadine holds my cheeks. Our faces draw closer. They call her "Freckles" at school, but to me her sandy specks glimmer. I lied before, we don't pash whenever we can. This will be our first kiss together. My first actual kiss. We peck each other on the lips, then she peels away, her hazel eyes searching my face, as if I have an aura to investigate, then she leans in once more. Could this be more than a peck? And then Star Wars guy opens his front door and we drop our hands away.

He half-grunts at us as he passes us by, B.O. aplenty.

Nadine laughs and pokes me in the stomach. "How embarrassing,"

"Yeah."

We discuss where we'll go. My place is a no-no too. For myriad reasons, I don't want her to meet Dad. Then I take the note out of my pocket. "For us."

"Shit."

"*We* are going to the movies."

"You work for that or is your dad pretty liberal with cash?"

"Nah, this old lady gave it to me. I told her all about us. She wanted to ensure that we both have a good time."

"You took money from an old lady?"

"A *loaded* old lady."

"Does it really matter? You took twenty bucks for what?" I think she picks up on my dismay. "We'll talk about it later."

I ask her whether she still wants to go and she says, "S'pose," so we head off.

It's only the two of us at the bus stop. She drapes an arm over mine.

"You ever have a dog?" I ask. "Would've loved one, myself. Always been on the move. Kind of crazy. New schools every year, sometimes twice a year."

"That's tough."

"And I'd really like to stay this time."

"Why's that?"

I squeeze her hand for a reply.

"Had to give Ricky up," Nadine says, "when mum couldn't afford the mortgage repayments at our house. Flats are apparently too small for a German Shepherd."

But I hear dogs barking all the time in the flats and I tell her such. Nadine explains that we're allowed dogs you can carry reasonably about the place. "You know, large rats."

"And Ricky?"

"Bawled my eyes out at the time. Moving sucks! And you, poor guy, have had to do it over and over."

"Do you go back to visit?"

Nadine's hands cradle the back of my head and reel me in for more than a peck. There's saliva and tongue involved—what I've yearned for, yet I discover I don't really know what to do and almost gag.

She pats my hand. "It'll get better, my young apprentice."

"That obvious?"

"Now it's time to fess up.'"

About what? My obvious inexperience? I clench up all over. *The twenty bucks? Surely, she's not on to dad?*
"Fess up?"

"Might be the wrong phrase. Look, I'm not using money you didn't earn to go to the movies. It doesn't gel with me."

I battle it out a bit, how I wanna go with her, and why waste the cash. After to-and-froing she comes up with: "How about we spend the twenty on her?"

"Dad and I take her out for lunch all the time." I want to add: *congealing the arteries* and *quickening the process*. If Dad knew I was with this moralistic do-gooder his own blood pressure would accelerate quicker than Allan Wells. And if Nadine knew the schemes my goblin dad and I had run in the past, she'd be bolting away from me even faster.

"That's sweet."

I let it ride. One thing Dad has taught me is that our fronts are mere illusions, but if you give the illusion some light it becomes a charm of sorts. Romanticizing our heists is a speciality of his.

"Where does she live?"

I tell her the swanky part of Mosman Park. Nadine stands up. "Well, come on then." And we cross over to the other side of the road to the deli and another bus stop, which heads away from the cinema. "How about we get some flowers for her? Everyone loves flowers."

I hand over the twenty, and she pops into the deli and grabs a bunch. "Gardenias and jonquils," she announces, and hands me back change. "Take a whiff. Not only beautiful but fragrant. Like my flowers to offer more than just good looks."

I sniff. "Like me," I say, trying to alleviate my own disappointment about not going to the movies.

"I like you, Andrew, but it's early days. I'll wait to see what your true fragrance is before I pass judgment."

You'd think the comment would disturb me, but it makes me want to impress her all the more.

Aunty has the gate open. And as soon as we enter, she'd brewing us tea. We help take vegemite, cheese and pickles on crispbreads to the garden table, with its million-dollar view of the Swan River. "My, aren't they beautiful!" she says regarding the flowers. She kisses Nadine and me over and again. And when Nadine returns to the kitchen to fetch the teas, Aunty gives me the thumbs-up. "She's beautiful. Think she's a keeper."

"You mean it?"

"Know what you're thinking—you're young. But that's the way life is sometimes."

When we're all gathered, Aunty opens up about her own husband. How they met at a dance when she was only twenty and promised to another. "It was like everybody else in the hall had vanished.'

"He must've been a real looker," I say into her ear. We have seated ourselves on either side of her—I've told Nadine how the secret to communicating with deaf types is to speak into their ear rather than roar away.

"Not in a traditional manner. More the James Cagney type."

We nod, clueless to who James Cagney is.

"Had something," says Aunty, "can't quite put my finger on it ... a warm spirit. Like you two: warm spirits."

We have one cuppa and then Aunty insists on another, and I worry that she'll insist on a third, *and* the sun will start to lower *and* I won't make it home *and* I'll be grounded. We continue to chat about Aunty's younger days, rolling into the Depression, only segueing when Nadine asks about pets. "Truth be known," says Aunty, "I miss Athos as much as I do my husband. Nobody is more like family than a dog. Kids won't let me get another one. Too much responsibility."

When we leave, Aunty thinks she's whispering in my ear, only on account of her ailing ears it's audible to Nadine, "I'll take care of you. Your future will be bright."

And then she holds out another twenty-dollar bill for us. "And this time don't you dare use it on me. You two get out there and have fun!'"

Nadine stiffens.

"I can't take it, Aunty," I say, "appreciate the gesture. All I wanted was for you and Nadine to meet."

"Rubbish," she says, and although she's on her walker she tries to stuff the note down my shirt.

Nadine, thanking Aunty, takes it before Aunty loses balance.

Nadine wants to hang out some more after the gates close behind us.

But as we take the bus to our stop the lowering sun is painting the clouds in citrus.

Speed Guy is outside the entrance to our flats trying to rip a drainpipe from the wall, growling four-letter expletives.

We keep back. It's a risk either way with the sun nearing the horizon. I am eager to be home for Dad. I always like to see that green flash, it cements who he is for me, but Speed Guy is in a frenzied whirl.

Nadine shrugs and suggests we go for a walk.

"Love to," I reply, "but I have to get home as soon as it's safe."

"What, you Cindy or something?"

"Cindy?"

"You know, Cind-e-rel-la."

I laugh and the words—*I love you*—come out before I know it; released from me at the same time Speed Guy pulls part of the pipe away, roaring away as he bloodies his hands. Distracted, we both dart inside without him noticing.

"I'll let you run off," Nadine kisses me on the cheek. "Make sure you leave a shoe behind. I'll search the Kingdom of Flats to see whose foot it fits." She grips me tight, blows warm air into my ear, "Think you're pretty cool too." Letting go, Nadine pulls out the twenty dollar note and puts it in my pocket. "As long as you spend it on Aunty."

I enter our home-for-now. Dad is hanging clothes off the railing on the sardine can of a balcony; lightsabers swish away in our neighbor's place.

I step outside to help.

"How'd you go?" winks Dad, holding up a pair of socks. "Charm the socks off her?"

"Sort of ... Actually, more the other way around."

"That's my boy," he interjects.

"By the way, careful venturing out. Speed Guy is on the rampage."

It's a tight squeeze getting the socks and undies in between the shirts, but we're well-practiced. "Can I talk to you? About something important."

"Not about staying on longer again?"

I shake my head. He asks me what's up.

"I can't go through with this. Not with Aunty. She made us tea. How can we be involved with someone who made Nadine and me tea?"

"What do you think we're doing, Andrew?"

"One of the old routines, Dad. Helping along the process."

"Really, Andrew? It's not like we're lining her liver with alcohol. All we're doing is showing her the time of her life. Who else has she got?"

"Colonel Kentucky?"

"Don't get smart."

"Dad, it's another scam. You've locked the will in. Ease up. Let nature take its course."

"You still don't get it, do you? We're not termites, Andrew. We don't get in there and destroy. We're your regular type of garden ants."

"We're ants now?"

"Garden ants—not Argentine ants, they're as bad as termites, not psycho ants with stingers, not warrior ants. Just the normal kind. The bore worm or beetle will tunnel through a frangipani; garden ants simply finish it off. If there's a wounded worm, we finish it off. If there's wood rotting away—"

"We finish it off. Get the pattern. And I'm not going to do it, not with Aunty. Not this time."

"But it's your nature, kiddo. Our nature."

"I'll be damned if it's in my nature."

"You can't escape who you are."

"I can rise above the depths you're stooping to."

He stops, face to the horizon, the sky now the yellows and oranges and reds of a peach skin. "Back in a tick. Don't move."

He tears off inside and then leaps back out with a hand mirror. He snatches my arm, twists me around so that my back is against his stomach, and lays his forearm around my chest so I can't squirm away. With the other hand, he holds the mirror out. "Look. Stay sharp. My dad gave me the same lesson, around the same age. See your rich inheritance."

"Interesting, Dad. What do garden ants inherit?"

He clasps me harder.

"Keep looking." And the sun lowers, sharper than usual. And as it goes below the horizon, I squeeze my lids shut and stomp on his foot.

"Ow. But there! You saw it didn't you?"

"Sure did, Dad." Although I didn't see squat.

"That's why we do what we do. You can't stop nature."

I nod, so he can release me.

As soon as the shops open the next morning, I'm picking up my list of necessities from the pet shop. I arrange to meet Nadine later at Aunty's.

And then it's off to greet my miniature mongrel mate.

A few hours later, although embarrassed by my recent evolution into a sweaty swamp monster, I ring the bell at Aunty's gate. I hope Nadine doesn't mind. Had to trek all the way in the humid sun, with a loaded backpack, and something else. Couldn't bring what I've brought otherwise.

Nadine comes out and is greeted by a white-tipped tail wagging and a yap or two. She jumps up and down, covers her mouth. He doesn't look like much, but I've put the mongrel through the ringer: flea-bathed him, new leash, collar around his neck. I couldn't prevent the smattering of red spots, remnants of tics removed with a treated needle, but instead of alcohol I used mercurochrome. Where on Earth do you get pure alcohol from? Dad's lagers wouldn't cut it, according to the pet store people.

The dog falls over at Nadine's feet. She kneels, gives him a good rub.

"What's his name?"

"Let's see what Aunty wants to call him."

Aunty is seated on the garden table, and I realise how I might not have thought this through. I suppose the dog is for Aunty, but it's also small enough for Nadine to keep in the flats. Little guy can be held in one arm, after all. I've brought some dog food and dog biscuits in my backpack.

Will he be accepted by society? Will he whine away in misery? But the guy seems to be having a ball; he's running around the yard, charging back for pats, and then he's off again.

"He's yours, Aunty," I say in her ear. "What should we call him? I can help out, if you'd like. Walk him and all that."

Aunty's eyes glisten, but she stays mute.

"Aunty?"

She pats my arm.

"What do you reckon, Aunty? Little Dingo? Prince? River? Pirate?"

Nadine chimes in. "Charlie? Or is he a Jack? Basil? Fido?"

Aunty finds her voice, "My kids are right," she says as our mongrel lifts a back paw and pees on a table leg. Thankfully, it's the far leg so the spray doesn't reach us. "I can't take care of him, Andrew."

"But I can help you, Aunty."

"Wish it were so," she replies. "Wish it were so."

"How about a name then, Aunty? We'll start there."

"I've got a name," says Aunty 'Want to hear it?"

We nod. Nadine slips her arm around mine.

"Andine. But the rule is he can't be called Andy for short. Has to be the full name. Deal?"

Takes a while to sink in; the combo reveals how much Aunty cares for us. It hardens my resolve to prevent Dad's ant work.

Before we leave, we put some dog food and water out, and give Andine plenty of lead so that he's got real space to roam around the yard. We haven't had enough time to ensure he can't squeeze under the palatial entrance gates. "He'll be right for a night," I say to Nadine, more for my own self-reassurance.

While we wash up the cups and saucers, I reflect over it all. Dad would never let me keep Andine—dogs being far more advanced than meal worms. But Nadine might be able to. Why is finding Andine a home is so important to me? What home am I really intending him to go to?

When we kiss Aunty goodbye, she's quiet, her farewell lacks the usual gutsy spark, but there's real feeling in her words: "Now listen, you two. You both take good care of each other. Do you hear me? Take real good care."

Outside of the gates, Nadine wraps her arms around me. "That was sweet, Andrew."

"Do you think she'll be able to keep him?"

"Of course not," she says and kisses my lips between sentences. Her breath is honey to me. "But it's so thoughtful. Small enough for the flats." My lips feel her nectar again. "You've thought it through! Visiting companion for Aunty and a new dog for me." This time we pash, and I don't gag, and I feel warm and wonderful. We keep kissing.

Then we make our way, my arm locked in hers, all the way to the bus stop.

• • •

It ended up being Aunty's final evening.

With this type of gig, on occasion, Dad and I attend the hospital. Especially when the families are not around. Dad will often hold a hand, while the death rattle occurs. It's a torturous sound, an inner heaving of a body pumping and struggling and clattering as the spirit leaves. Thankfully, Aunty died in her sleep.

Dad wears his Sunday best to the funeral. The family are all appreciative of his presence; how Aunty spoke so fondly of us in this her final year: "Wonderful lunches", "Plenty of laughs and smiles". In a couple of months' time, when the will is read, that'll change. The papers will be contested of course. Cursing and hate mail and threats. Dad will settle for some kind of deal and then blow it, like he always does, and then it'll be another scam someplace else.

A new home with no Nadine.

There's no Andine either ... He vanished. Dad claimed when he arrived at Aunty's home, our mongrel was gone. "I swear it! Family never saw him. Either he chewed through the leash or Aunty released him. Kind of symbolic, I suppose. Maybe he left when she passed?"

I don't know where the truth lies with my goblin dad. Probably set Andine "free" himself.

The following week is especially precious. I don't burden Nadine with the knowledge I'm leaving. I savor every outing, every laugh—and notwithstanding the grief, there are laughs. I also meet her mum on a Good Day, we listen to songs by The Village People, Split Enz, and The Pretenders, walk by the river, think of Aunty, think of Andine, navigate around Speed Guy, make lame Vader and Jedi jokes about the other neighbor.

And armed with repellent, Nadine twice braves the river mire and marshes with me. Nadine doesn't whinge about it either, her only complaint is how our searches proved fruitless.

Nadine and me. I know now what love is.

The one thing we never do is spend a sunset together.

You can't really call it dropping the bomb, since it's expected, but it's a bomb nevertheless. Dad's all cliché central: "Hey, son," "Know it's hard." "You mean the world to me," and later that arvo, as it nears sunset, it's, "Have your bags packed. We're leaving in the morning."

For a moment I think of running off—which has proven pretty ineffectual before—but dad has situated himself by the door.

"Not anymore," I declare. "No more scheming."

My face must appear as raw as it feels, because Dad hugs me. "No oldies, not again. We'll only hit scumbags from now on. How's that sound?" He brushes my wet cheeks with his T-shirt. "Next gig is the greyhound industry. It's good work. Bit risky, but we'll bribe the shit out of them. And if they don't pay, we'll sell the footage to the current affair shows. Think of it—educational, we'll be filming, creating a story—and fun stuff: espionage work. We'll be spies on the right side."

It sounds convincing, but Nadine and lost-Andine anchor me down. "I love her, Dad. Know you think I'm too young for it, but I love her. Like really love her. And she loves me."

The sun is falling in the background. "We can't take her with us. But how about you write and see how it goes?"

As the sun sets, Dad is briefly sheened in emerald. *Goblin*. "Can't take you away from the heist, hey Dad? Garden ant and all."

"We can't change our legacy, Andrew."

"No more elderly?"

"Promise."

"It's a deal, if you let me say bye to Nadine."

"Sure thing. You know I love you, Andrew. Be back in an hour. Early start. I'll have a hot cocoa ready for you when you come back."

•

Nadine's mum is having another off day, so we sit on the staircase.

"You can look at me," she says.

I peer up from the step under my feet. I want to be dramatic, thump away like Speed Guy, show the incense. But Nadine has grown me.

"We're moving again."

She puts her arm over my shoulder. I know her face will be tearing up like my own.

The Star Wars nerd descends the stairs and stops by us. "Couldn't help overhearing. You two okay?"

He's human after all. We all smile sad smiles.

"Leia and Luke were from different sides of the galaxy but were brought together by a common cause."

"What does that even mean?" I say. And the more charitable Nadine simply says, "Thanks."

"Let me try again. Darth Vader told Luke that the Dark Side was his destiny, but Luke never surrendered." He pats me on my back.

As he rolls on down the stairs, he's left behind a more fortified me.

...

The first few weeks in Northam are rough. I keep thinking of Nadine, and then Andine; and Aunt Rose, who visits me in my dreams, is never far away either.

Northam's main strip has some history, but it's a dodgy town, with plenty of people around to give Speed Guy a run for his money; an array of down-and-outs, looking to spiral further downward rather than upward: glue and petrol and substance sniffers, street alcoholics. Settling into the new high school is hard, too; fights every day, each one surrounded by a ring of students.

But it's not all bad. The library has become a place of sanctuary, and like any rural place, there's enough grounded approachable types about, but I just don't know whether it's worth making friends. Dad will already have plans in motion. Irony is he's losing a stack at the "dogs"—the very place he wants to bribe or bring down.

Nadine and I write and call. Being apart is scary. I wonder if her letters are getting shorter, whether there's less to talk about on the phone, whether Dad will continue to let me rack up the phone bill.

Then one afternoon, I get a letter. *Caught a glimpse of Andine. Haven't been telling you, but I've been going down to the marshes.*

The very next morning, I drop off a letter to meet me in three days' time, by the marshes at 4 p.m.

I head for the train station. Left a note on the kitchen bench for Dad, too; don't know how much time it'll give me, but it has the lines: *I'm heading off to Kalgoorlie for a while to find myself. And if you send anyone, I'll call the Avon Valley Greyhound Racing Association and blow your cover.* I end it with: *Hope you're proud of me—on a scheme of my own. Love, Andrew.*

I don't know what I'll do for the night, but that's a risk I'm willing to take. I'm not naïve, I know I'll find myself back in Northam with Dad sooner rather than later.

I trudge through the marshlands. Ten minutes late. No sign yet of Nadine. And the sky is steadily glooming. Flies and mozzies, more abundant than ever, swarm all over me. And then I hear a voice yelling my name. It's most unlike Nadine to yell, which makes it all the sweeter. And suddenly it's as if the flies and mozzies are silent and the stench has vanished.

"He's out there," she says after we hug forever.

"We'll find him."

We resume our search. Being in the morasses becomes real again: we scratch our many bites, hold sleeves over our noses when the reek is too evil, swat away buzzing insects, get pricked by pointed stems piercing our jeans.

There's a series of barks.

Andine arrives, more like he was before the cleanup, but though the leash is long gone, the collar is intact. We bend over him and pat away, until we're as covered in grime as he is. The drab earth is all rainbows and butterflies.

But then Andine darts away. We shout his name. He briefly turns back, before charging off into the swamplands. I want to fall to the ground, roll around, really coat myself in muck. What does it all mean?

"He'll be back," says Nadine.

"Really think so?"

"I'm certain."

I know Nadine can't be so assured. Nobody, after all, can guarantee an unforeseen future. Meanwhile, she takes my hand and leads me out of the marshes. The sun lowers further.

We exit the swamp and approach a bench on a grassed area overlooking the river.

I park myself on the bench, patting the empty space next to me. "Sit down?"

"Shouldn't we wash up a bit first?"

I shake my head. "I want us to be together while the sun sets." My voice is feigned confidence. Reality is, I am doing all I can to prevent my vocal cords and limbs from tremoring.

She shrugs and sits by my side. "And watch me carefully as the sun dips below the horizon."

■

Anthony Panegyres' stories have appeared in The Best Australian Stories, The Year's Best Australian Fantasy & Horror Vol. 2 & 6, Overland Literary Journal 204 & 214, Meanjin Quarterly, *the award-winning anthologies* Bloodlines *and* At the Edge *and elsewhere. His most recent story homes include the anthologies:* We'll Stand in That Place & Other Stories; The Sky Falls Down: An Anthology of Loss; Changing Tides, *and* Spawn of War and Deathiness. *He has been shortlisted for a number of awards, including The Aurealis Award for Best Fantasy Story. Although more comfortable with prose, he has also had nonfiction published on the* Overland *and* Meanjin *websites and in* The Guardian. *His previous* Bourbon Penn *story, "Anthropophages Anonymous (AA)" was in BP 25, and earned a mention in Ellen Datlow's yearly list of recommended stories.*

THERE ARE ONLY TWO CHAIRS, AND THE SKIN IS DRAPED OVER THE OTHER

■

Alexia Antoniou

Behind Catherine's house is a stream that smells like hard-boiled eggs.

There is also a white iron table so orange with rust it looks like someone had a pizza party on it without any plates, and two white iron chairs to go with the table, and a netless soccer goal.

But the stream is what is important and what is interesting about Catherine's backyard.

The stream brings us presents. Sprite bottles – the glass kind – and magazines with all the pages wet and stuck together, ink so blurry you can hardly tell what's a boob and what's an elbow (Catherine lets me take these home, where I spend a lot of time trying to Find a Nipple.) There is one very exciting time when the stream brings us a toy boat, the kind a little kid would take to the beach, and at the bottom of the boat is a key on a hard plastic keyring with a picture of a pig on it winking and saying HOGWILD.

But for the most part, the presents the stream brings us are objectively trash.

Catherine and I do not mind. We've been interested in the stream for a long time now, since at least the third grade.

It's the summer before eighth now. We hang out back there and pretend that we are very lost, that we have to follow the water back to Civilization. Catherine likes to lick her lips behind me and I like to pretend I don't see her lifting a heavy wet tree branch so she can knock me out and eat my butt meat for survival.

We hang out back there and pretend that Catherine is a water nymph who has seduced and drowned my husband, just for fun, and I like to scream and pummel her chest with my fists until we tumble into the water, which is shallow and weirdly warm.

Something about the stream makes our hair dry hard and stinky. Catherine's mom breaks three teeth off a plastic pink comb one night trying to help us brush it out. We give up and eat pizza bagels in front of the TV with the comb still dangling from Catherine's hair. My mom has asked Catherine's mom many, many times to not let me play back there, but Catherine's mom does not seem to know how to stop us. She does, however, make us put a towel across our pillows to protect the pillowcases while we sleep.

One day, while we are pretending that the stream behind Catherine's house is a Holy Stream and that Catherine is my mother, dragging my small and awful body by the armpits to be healed, the stream brings us a new kind of present.

Catherine sees it first, of course.

"Oh, gross," she says, and drops me, which I do not like.

I roll onto my stomach and grab for her ankle, but then I see the thing that she sees in the stream and I let her shake me off.

It is ... confusing in a bad way to look at.

Half of it is in the water and half of it is out, pooling and folding over itself on the mud-and-gravel shore at Catherine's feet. It is very, very smooth, the color of chewed gum – and, as Catherine said, immediately gross. I want it not to be here. But since it *is* here ... I want Catherine to touch it. Which she does, holding it dripping from the water like the worst laundry.

"It's heavy," she says, "really heavy."

And even though I know that it is impossible to see the stream from inside Catherine's house, because it is down a little bit of a hill, I still check over my shoulder. It feels like we are doing something so unallowed that no one has ever had to say in words that we are not supposed to do this.

"It's got a belly button," I finally say (because it does.)

"I hate you," Catherine says, "That's so gross."

We identify:

-several moles, including one like half a grape tucked inside what is clearly an armpit

-little cuts, practically everywhere, that flap pinkly at us but don't actually bleed

-and the vulva.

This is not a word we say out loud – we just make very disgusted eye contact and Catherine says, "oh my *god*," and I roll onto my back and cover my whole face.

I don't want to keep looking at the skin. So I just stay like that, on my back. I try to focus on the places where I am lying on a stick or on a rock, picturing, in my head, little blue exclamation points pinging above my body where it hurts. I try to focus on the sky, which is so white it makes behind my eyes feel fuzzy. But what I hear is Catherine, who won't stop noticing things out loud.

"There is, like, *no hair*. Anywhere. No tan lines either. That's weird, right? We should be writing this down."

And then she says, "I *really* don't like its face."

And because this time her voice is so tight and so small and so high that I feel it in my own chest, I sit up and look at her.

She is holding what is, terribly, the face of the skin. She's got it spread across her two hands, holding it with her fingertips like she's about to play cat's cradle. She is staring softly through wetly clumped lashes into the empty holes that must be the skin's eyes.

So I stand up, and I bite her.

Just on the arm, and it's mostly sleeve in my mouth anyway. But Catherine yells and drops the skin into the water, which is good, even if the noise it makes while falling is all wrong – a sucking-and-or-gasping sound I can't tell if Catherine even catches in her anger.

"You promised to stop doing that," she says. She is clutching her arm so dramatically away from me that she is bent almost in half.

I say, "Yeah."

But I am looking at the skin. Beneath the water – beneath the leaves and the dead dragonfly and the empty sweet-and-sour chip bag – the stream is bubbling through the hole that is the skin's mouth, opening it and closing it again and again and again so that it looks like it is saying something.

• • •

That night, Catherine and I do not talk about what happened at all. Which is weird for us.

We come inside to wash our hands and find that Catherine's younger brother has gotten a very good grade on his final report card or has won a contest or maybe it's his half birthday; there is a party feeling all around us during dinner, and after dinner, strawberry sheet cake with strawberry frosting. I am delicately wrapping a second square of cake in a paper towel to take to Catherine's room when I hear Catherine ask who wants to play Scrabble.

Now I know she is avoiding being alone with me.

I sit on the tight carpet floor of the den and watch Catherine's family play Scrabble. I pick cat hair out of the carpet and keep track of the points – I am not allowed to play because I only ever make up words – and because I am keeping track of the points, Catherine wins by a *lot*. She even tries to get a second game going but, mercifully, we are made to go to bed by Catherine's mom.

I try to catch Catherine's eyes in the mirror while we are brushing our teeth, but she is only looking at herself.

"Catherine," I whisper directly into her face when we are finally in her bed. The yellow sheet, gray in the dark, is pulled all the way to her chin, and she is making a face I can tell she thinks is a sleeping face, but is actually more like the face a teacher makes while going, "Well, how old do you *think* I am," (but with her eyes closed.)

I touch my forehead to her forehead and whisper again, "*Catherine.*"

"Stop," she says. And I can tell from her voice that I am being too much.

I roll as far away from her on the twin-sized bed as I possibly can, howling in my body long after Catherine's thick breathing tells me she's actually asleep.

The next morning, Catherine has a dentist appointment. I wake up alone in her bedroom and am out behind her house in ten minutes, wearing a big soft shirt of Catherine's and a pair of my own gym shorts that I find folded up in her dresser.

The egg smell rising up from the stream is powerful. I creep past the rusted white iron table, finishing my square of leftover strawberry cake, and I creep past the netless soccer goal and I creep past the chairs, all of which are pearled over with humidity. The cicadas are making their alarm bell noise but otherwise everything is just silent and soggy, even the pine needles so wet they're unpokeful on my bare feet.

I am slow and careful walking down the almost-hill. And the skin is not in the stream.

...

I do not see Catherine for a few days; my mom thinks it is healthy for me to live at our house and sleep in my bed and have dinner together every now and then. But I call Catherine a lot on the phone, and some of the times she answers and some of the times she does *not* – which makes my stomach hurt.

"Why do you think that happened to us," I ask over the phone.

It is our second call of the day, a little after lunch. It's been cloudy since morning, all dark and very still, and with the lights off in our house it almost feels like I am hiding. I am sitting against the wall in the hallway, curled ammonite-like over the phone so that my mom (who is peeling apples over the kitchen trash can) does not hear. My mouth is chalky and my breath bouncing off the receiver smells like mixed berry antacid tablets; I almost ask Catherine if she can smell it.

"Never you mind," she says.

I hang up on her.

And then I call her back. She's taken the phone off the hook, which is annoying and just like her, so I tell my mom I am going for a bike ride and when she asks me where to, I say to hell. And I ride over to Catherine's.

Even without the sun, the air outside is hot. The whole ride over, it feels like a big animal is breathing down on me and I am sweating by the time I get to Catherine's house.

I dump my bike in Catherine's driveway, which is empty. Her yard is droopy with purple coneflowers, at every center a bee circling like a dizzy moon. I cross the buzzing yard and I pass along the side of Catherine's house, where the windows are all half-open. I can hear her brother (or someone else who is just okay at piano) practicing the same tripping notes over and over again.

And behind her house, Catherine waits for me with the skin.

"Hi," she says, "You took forever."

They are sitting at the white iron table, or at least, Catherine is sitting, swirling a wine glass full of water very close to her eyes. It's stream water, I can tell, yellowish and full of dirt and bug parts that twirl in Catherine's hand. A second wine glass sits dripping on the table.

I look at Catherine and I look at the skin. I look behind me into the dark kitchen window, where nobody is watching us. Sweat is finding the open bug bites in the spaces behind my knees, but I don't itch them and I don't say anything until Catherine puts her wine glass on the table and closes one eye at me in a way I know means she is concentrating.

"I think we should be careful about whatever we're about to do," I say.

(Or at least, I think it.)

"Come here," she says.

I do not want to. There are only two chairs, and the skin is draped over the other. Its neck is hanging down the backrest and I cannot see its face.

But I come over to Catherine and – so that she doesn't think she can just tell me what to do – I pick up her wine glass and I drink about half of it in one strong gulp.

"You're so stupid," she says.

But she is smiling at me. She is smiling at me hard and the skin in the chair beside her is leaking water from all these little cuts in thin, clear streams. Catherine moves and I sit on her armrest, leaning against her arm. It's surprisingly cold but still a little sweaty.

I try not to touch my tongue to the soft bits of bug that are caught between my teeth.

And as I watch, a fly lands just below the skin's knee; it crawls, unswatted, down and around an unfilled shin.

To be honest, the next few weeks are a little weird. Catherine insists that the skin is a part of every game we play now, which I have feelings about, even if I can't tell exactly what they are.

We hang out by the stream behind Catherine's house and pretend that the skin is Catherine's teacher, a wizard, who's made a terrible mistake resulting in flatfulness that only her apprentice, Catherine, can fix.

We hang out by the stream behind Catherine's house and pretend that the skin is a very ugly kind of demon that Catherine must outsmart in increasingly dangerous battles of wit. When the skin is defeated, I make it stomp its feet and shake its fists and throw itself down in the mud in despair over having lost Catherine's precious soul. It is a relief, getting to drop the skin; it's so much longer than me and heavy in my arms, and I find myself playing it more and more often.

One night, alone in my room, I write in my journal: I am its muscles and its bones.

I am not, I don't think, its mouth – which is something I can't tell if Catherine knows yet. I will say things, I mean, and I am saying them with my tongue and with my voice, but the words feel like the fruit of a seed planted deep inside me when I wasn't looking. Like, when the demon is supposed to be asking Catherine riddles. The first time we play, I ruin everything because I cannot stop saying, "When is the glimmering and when is the spider," and, "Who did this," and "Who did this," (again), until finally Catherine says, whatever *this* is, she isn't feeling it, and I get upset and end up biking home.

Like I said, a little weird but not, I think, a big deal.

Until one day, while we are not pretending anything but are just sitting beside the stream trying to feed a cheese puff to a crow, I find myself telling Catherine that I would like to dance with her.

Which is not something I have ever wanted to say.

The skin, at that moment, is hanging in the tree above us, folded over a branch so that all of its fingers are reaching down. Gravity is pulling at the holes that are its eyes and the holes that are its mouth so they are very, very open, and I am telling Catherine over and over in a voice so low I can barely hear it myself that I would like to dance with her, I would like to dance with her, I would like to dance with her so, so, so, so much.

It's terrible but I can't stop. Not even with Catherine looking at me and frowning with just her eyebrows.

"I would like to dance with you," I say again, and feel like a creep.

Catherine wipes her hands on her shorts. I watch her stand and take one of the skin's dangling hands between her own.

"You want to dance with me," she says. And because she is looking at her hands and what they are holding, it isn't super clear who she is talking to.

My heart in my chest is beating fast enough to actually hurt. Even the crunch of the mud and gravel beneath my feet as I stand makes me feel jumpy. Jumpy in my cells, like my outline is fizzing. Catherine tugs and the whole of the skin slips over the branch and into her arms. It makes a sound as it falls like a sheet being shook. I think of my mom, suddenly, making the bed with me still in it when I was very little. And then I come and I take the skin from Catherine.

She's frowning at me, still. I hold the skin by its empty wrists. I move our hands and I place them on Catherine's hips. The head of the skin falls backward over my shoulder.

I don't look at it.

There is still so much space between Catherine and me.

The legs of the skin are too long between us and there's nowhere that our feet can really go, so we just stand there – the three of us – for what feels like a really, really, really long time.

And that night, I imagine, I will rise from my bed.

I will walk from my bed to the window between my desk and my closet and my footsteps will be invisible-quiet in the carpet. I will press a line of me – my forehead, my nose, my shoulder – against the glass, and the curtain will spill down my back like a wedding veil.

And in the street, there'll be Catherine. She'll be standing just outside the circle of light from my neighbor's garage, and she'll be holding herself by the elbows, embarrassed and very hard to see.

She'll be wearing the skin.

I'll still know it's her. I'll raise my hand up to the glass like, *hey*.

∎

This is Alexia Antoniou's first short story – but if you like her writing, she thinks you might also enjoy her folk duo, Gawain and the Green Knight! Look for it and for her at GawainandtheGreenKnightBand.com

TONE DEAF

———————— ■ ————————

Corey Farrenkopf

Someone bought the old church in South Chatham. They took down the cross, stripped all mention of Jesus from the front bulletin by the edge of Route 28. Stained glass still bled crimson at noon, windows still tucked between black shutters, white clapboard still spotted with moss. Mark, Cashel, and I watched from the other side of the street as two men dredged sun-yellowed paperbacks from the Christian free library shed on the property, piling them in a temporary dumpster in the parking lot.

"Not big on recycling," I whispered.

Mark shook his head, adjusting his light blue baseball cap.

"What are you guys doing with the place?" Cashel called.

One of the men paused, looking over his shoulder, mouth open as if he couldn't place the words. Without responding, the man waved his free hand, goading us to leave as he balanced a banker's box of books with the other.

"Dude, it's an easy question," Mark added. "Are we talking about another church? A private residence? Maybe a nightclub?"

"Go," the man said in a thick accent none of us could place, fully turning, muscles thick beneath baggy clothes. He dropped the box, the cardboard sides splitting, spilling Bibles and out-of-print *Lives of Saints* across the parking lot.

"Okay, cool, whatever," I replied, dropping my skateboard to the sidewalk. "They'll put up a sign."

"True," Cashel said, as he got on his own skateboard, pushing off, coasting down the hill toward the post office. Mark and I followed, careful as we crossed humped tree roots bisecting the pavement.

It had been over a month, and no one had put up a sign.

We hoped they'd do what they did in Yarmouth with the New Church. Turn it into a concert venue, high ceilings creating lush reverb for punk bands and noise rock groups. The Village Hall next door used to let us rent the space for shows, but someone carved a penis into a windowsill, and now they have a strict no-concert policy. The same thing happened at the Eastham Elks Lodge, and the Senior Center, and the old Rec Center. It was always a penis, graffitied on some wall, that ruined youth culture.

Almost all the venues on Cape Cod had gone under or closed to anyone below the age of sixty-five. Bingo nights were okay. Meat raffles, too. The New Church was the only option, but they didn't have heat, so it was a seasonal thing.

The three of us, like everyone on the peninsula, needed something to drag us through the gray of winter when all the shops and restaurants catering to tourists closed.

We'd all decided to take a gap year before college, Mark's father offering us jobs at his flooring company. Some days we installed oak in refinished dining rooms, others we sold tile from the show room. I enjoyed going to different job sites, seeing the insane money people pumped into old cottages by the water, but the salesman stuff wasn't my thing. I barely knew the product. Could never find the right pitch. It was just one year, then

I'd head to Western Mass and get a degree in biology or botany or something that wouldn't involve selling linoleum to strangers.

"Think we should knock?" Mark asked.

"I think if we were meant to understand it, they'd write in English," Cashel added.

The new owners had finally done something to the sign out front, slipping letters into the pre-spaced grooves. The language didn't resemble any I was familiar with. Mark took a picture with his iPhone, ran it through an image search that kicked back no results. There were a lot of vowels, few consonants beyond Qs and Rs.

"Maybe it's a Norwegian Death Metal thing? Those guys love making up languages," Mark said.

"I could live with that," I replied.

Metal was only two steps removed from punk. Maybe they'd let our band open shows? Get the crowd going. Regardless, anything was better than another bingo hall timesharing with square-dance instructors.

"So, you're going to knock?" Cashel asked, prodding the back of my thigh with his skateboard.

"I guess," I replied.

We crossed the street, but I traced the front path alone, passing beneath overgrown maples, their gray branches leafless in late autumn. Through the front window, the space looked abandoned, lights mute, no sounds drifting from within. Squinting, I could make out what looked like a new flat screen television above the altar, replacing the crucifix that had hung there.

The TV played the Netflix equivalent of ambient rock, a starscape, constellations wavering, pinpricks of light bleeding through tubes and diodes designed to calm someone as they studied for a test or wanted to set the mood for a Tinder date. It was weird to see the night sky hanging there, flickering above the pews, backset by boards in the ceiling. They'd left the lectern, draped with dark cloth, a bowl of fruit perched on top. Pomegranates maybe? Something with seeds and nodes and pulpy flesh.

I felt like a voyeur pressing my face to uncurtained windows. So, I knocked. The three rapped notes echoed through the space. I leaned an ear toward the door, searching for footsteps, a gruff reply from inside, but nothing came.

Again, I dragged my eyes through what I could see. Taking in the shaded pews, the few remaining candelabras, the starscape covering the wall, lens shifting, panning slowly to the left as if mapping the rotation of a distant galaxy. It was nuts to think humans had reached that point with technology, that satellites could filter images back from such distances.

I knocked again.

And again.

And again, but no one answered.

I considered trying the door handle to see if it was open but couldn't bring myself to turn the knob.

My parents' garage was half metal-bending shop, half recording studio. On the left stood two-ton metal shears, finger breaks, racks of sheet steel, and all the massive iron tools my father needed to create copper chimney caps and stove surrounds. The scent of oil lubricants and battery acid filled the space. On the other side stood the drum set and a wall of cheap amps we'd assembled from garage sales. A dozen patterned rugs blanketed the cement floor, attempting to absorb sound like the swaths of foam we hung from the walls. It wasn't an ideal setup, but it was the only place we could have band practice, and if we hoped to get our CD finished before our year was up, we had to work with what we had.

Before we retired the band, we needed proof of its existence beyond a shitty four-track demo.

It took forever to get drum and bass tracks aligned. Cashel played too fast, cymbals crashing at inopportune moments while I missed notes, strings squealing from pressure. Being tone deaf didn't help. I relied on my bandmates to assure me that, *yes, that was a G or an F flat.*

Cashel and I followed the readout on the computer screen, sharing a pair of earbuds, searching for a weak spot.

Mark tuned his Telecaster, sitting on a stool besides the wall of amps. He only used a distortion pedal, nothing else to vary tone. We were a standard punk band, no D-beats or breakdowns. More skatepunk than anything else.

"Are we good?" Mark asked.

"I think so," I replied. "You ready?"

"Of course," Mark said.

Cashel pressed record and the metronome counted in. The distortion was thick, palm muted through the intro, dragging into ringing chords for the chorus. Before Mark could get through the bridge, my father's fire radio whirred into life, bleating out tones reminiscent of a dying bird. In addition to bending metal, my father was also a firefighter and that wasn't the first time I'd forgotten to shut off his radio. He had one in every room of the house.

Overtime was how he made his money.

He couldn't miss a tone.

Mark swore, dialing down the volume knob as the dispatcher's voice cut from the radio.

"Dude, again? Really? You're supposed to turn that off," Mark said, shaking his head.

"I know, I know. Listen though," I replied.

Neighbors called in flames through the windows and roof at 2550 Main Street. Ladder and pump are on the scene. Calling for two for coverage ... the electric voice droned.

"Isn't that the church?" Cashel asked.

"I think so," I replied.

"You want to check it out?" Mark asked.

"You know my dad hates it when we show up," I said.

"We'll take my car," Cashel said.

"He knows what your car looks like," I replied.

"Just duck down when we pass. We'll pretend you aren't in the back seat," Mark said.

The fire wasn't in the church. It was in the old library shed out back. Smoke wept through a gash in the roof, its twin windows ringed black with soot. The door had been hacked inward, an ax blade shearing through lock and hinge as the crew searched for bodies. The flames were smothered by the time we got there, my father's coworkers coiling hoses, retracting ladders. The air reeked of smoke and burnt plastic and something acrid and sour. I could taste it, metal on my tongue, something organic crisped and bubbling.

"You think they knocked a candle over?" Mark asked.

"Don't know. But that thing's getting condemned," Cashel said. "I bet they'll knock it down in a week."

But they didn't knock it down in a week. The new owners let the blackened carcass stand, patching windows and doors with plywood, the pale wood becoming scar tissue against the charred siding. One of the doors had makeshift hinges. Someone still moved in and out, despite the carcinogenic issues and the orange X painted on all four sides.

No one had boarded over the wound in the roof, though, two-by-fours split, pressing through the hole like shattered ribs. It didn't so much look like one of the firefighters had hacked into the shingles as something had crashed through them, dropping from a great height to bring the building low.

My father said there was no known cause for the fire, no accelerant discovered. The entire inside had been stripped before flames licked up the walls.

"So, what did you write in the incident report?" I asked.

"Unknown. N/A. Something like that," he replied. "If it's not arson and no one died, we don't look much beyond that."

"But don't you want to know?" I asked.

"I've been to enough fires. They're usually more boring than you'd think."

"I thought you said there was a huge TV," Cashel said, pressing his face to the window.

"Yeah, above the altar," I replied.

The three of us stood on the front step, Mark having joked about my weak forearms and knocking proficiency. It was a gray day, the sky low, a hint of snow in the air. The road behind us was dead. Winter had called snowbirds back to Florida or Jersey or whatever warmer state they lived in half the year. Only locals were left.

"Well, there's nothing up there," Cashel said.

"Are you kidding me, the thing was huge," I replied, pushing Cashel aside, peering in. Above the altar, the cross was back, hanging from the wooden slats where the television had been. There was no way they would have put something that large up just to take it down. It was practically a movie theater screen, something you couldn't purchase at Best Buy.

"See," Cashel said.

"Yeah, but that's insane," I replied.

"How about we knock and just ask them? I'm starting to think there's no way we're playing a show here," Mark said.

"I'm thinking that's a hard pass," Cashel said, knocking against the door's glass window.

Only a faint electric hum came from within, but nothing human. After a moment, there was the stutter of steps from around back. We looked at each other, then jogged around the side of the building. The parking lot and burnt library came into view. The plywood door was open. A man hurried to close it, carrying what looked like a split pomegranate on a silver platter. The three of us edged back toward the church, clinging close to the wall, watching as the man disappeared through the back door.

"Is it like their food pantry or something?" Mark asked as we neared the sidewalk.

"Food pantries don't take perishables. Stuff goes bad," I said.

"And that thing looked raw as hell," Cashel said.

"The pomegranate?" I asked.

"There's no way that thing's a pomegranate. It was practically beating," Cashel said.

"Should we go look, or call someone?" I asked.

"Nope. We're just going to walk away and come back at night," Mark said.

"Night's always the right idea," Cashel replied.

Cashel was going to school in Ohio. Mark in PA. That's why we decided to call it quits with the band. It would be a struggle. We'd get rusty, hands no longer remembering chords, which solo went where, lyrics wilting and mumbled. We'd seen other bands try to keep up long-distance relationships. They went from headlining shows to becoming opening acts, only a small crowd of old friends there to watch. The aging process wasn't graceful in the scene.

That's why we needed the CD. Proof of five years of effort. Fifteen years of friendship. We weren't going to be sleeping over at each other's houses every Friday night, waking groggy on couch cushions, the scent of greasy pizza and weed in the air. And that made me sad. We'd marked our weeks with band practice, movie trips, shows in Boston, and the occasional sushi run to Yarmouth. We were what each other looked forward to at the end of the week, something to push through another day of sanding floors, of trying to convince retired couples they really wanted the high-end tile.

The church seemed like a final adventure, something to mark our passage from youth, arriving at our next instar.

"You going to hit the right notes this time?" Cashel asked as we recorded vocals.

"It's punk. As long as I'm close, it's fine," I replied, lips brushing the mic hovering before me.

"This is why we should have paid for lessons," Mark said. He'd pushed for voice lessons, but they were pricey, and we barely had time between work and our self-imposed recording schedule.

We'd all crowded into my parents' bathroom to do the vocals. With the lower ceilings and the tile, the sound was more manageable, crisp. Mark sat on the edge of the bathtub, while Cashel clicked keys on the laptop, sitting cross-legged on the black-and-white checkered floor.

"Maybe for the reunion tour I'll spring for it," I replied.

"Or maybe you'll just grow out of being tone deaf," Cashel said with a smile.

"That would be a blessing," Mark said.

Truthfully, my concentration was shot. I couldn't stop thinking about the guy cradling the pomegranate and the shed. Two weeks had passed, and we hadn't worked up the nerve to go back, only driving by at night, watching the crimson-tinted light slipping from inside. They only gathered after sundown, the few shadowed figures we glimpsed from a distance.

"I think tonight's the night," I said.

Cashel and Mark looked at me askew.

"Once I know what's going on over there, I'll be able to record, be more focused. You guys can't tell me you don't hear it? That humming?" I asked.

"Maybe," Mark said.

"I do hate lingering mysteries," Cashel said.

"Conveniently, you're both wearing black," I replied, pointing to their band T-shirts and skinny jeans. For the most part, all we ever wore was black. "No one has to run home to swap out a jacket."

"I'm passing," Cashel said, looking away.

"I'm with him, man. We've got work tomorrow and that shit was real sketchy last time," Mark said.

A distance grew between us, a near-translucent being rising from the floor, cold, sucking air from my throat. We rarely diverged. I knew they wanted to know as badly as

I did, but I could hear the fear in their voices. My hands shook. Nothing was going to get better until I knew what was going on in the church. Months were ticking by. We had three songs done out of twelve and the mistakes piled up. Hours burned before us.

"Let's just get it over with. We're going to go inside eventually. It's inevitable. You have to hear it calling," I said.

"Not me man, not a word," Mark said.

"Just drop it. I'm not getting slapped with trespassing over this," Cashel said.

"Focus on the song. Let's give it another go and we'll call it a night," Mark said, hand toying with the curtain.

"I can't," I said, stepping away from the mic, leaving them in my parents' bathroom as I dropped down the stairs to the first floor. They knew how to get out.

It had begun to snow. A thin skin of white coated the parking lot and sidewalk. My footprints marked my path to the front door, clear against the grimy cement beneath.

Like any good church, the door was unlocked. I didn't knock. I figured any denomination was happy to receive a new congregant, even if they arrived unannounced. The air inside the building was sweltering, the starscape back, obscuring the cross, TV rehung, pinpricks of orbiting light looming above the altar. I couldn't recognize the constellations, couldn't place the planets I'd always known. A man stood beneath the void, raising a platter with the pomegranate on it, as if making an offering to a digital god. I tried to speak, but couldn't find my tongue, words thick in my throat.

There were a dozen other men seated in the pews, staring blankly at the starscape, mouths twitching through words too low to hear. The pomegranate floated off the plater, rising toward the screen, which wasn't a screen. It wavered as the fruit passed into the night sky, rising and rising, muting stars as it obscured their view.

"Have you come to pray?" a voice asked from my side.

I turned.

Another man stood beside the door, nearly identical to the man on the altar, to all the men gathered in the pews. Head shaved to stubble, mouth lolling wide, wider than his jaw should have allowed.

I stuttered through an incoherent reply. "No, I ah, just wanted to ..."

"First you must make an offering," the man said, hand clutching my shoulder. "Come, you will find joy here."

I tried to pull away, to jerk from his grip, but he was strong, fingertips pressing between muscles, tunneling toward bone. He led me outside, into the cold December air, snow coming down harder than before. He dragged me around the corner of the church, feet slipping in the slush. A single candle flickered on the stone step leading to the burnt library. The door was ajar. I had told myself I wanted to see inside, but not like that, not without choice. The man pushed open the door as I fought to knock him off the step. He didn't flinch.

"Pluck the fruit and bring it to me," the man said, tossing me into the cinder-thick interior, the overwhelming scent of char and ash searing my sinuses. The walls were jet black, charcoal. The light from the doorway only reached so far, leaving the scarred walls in half shadow. A single spotlight fell through the wound in the ceiling, landing on the edge of something still, snow gathering around its base. There was my breath, and the man's breath, and another breath farther inside. I looked for an unboarded window, another door, but there was nothing. No exit.

"It doesn't hurt them. It's what they've come to do," the man said behind me. "Just tear one free. They don't understand pain."

"What doesn't?" I asked.

"They."

In the corner, the shadows stirred in the moonlight. The thing was an amalgam of so many things. Flora and fauna crossbred. Legs akin to a horse, head boorish, the trunk of a dozen small trees twisting off its bloated body, some drifting into the floor as if it were impaled on bamboo spikes. There was no way it could walk or drag itself out of the shed. Hundreds of spherical growths sprouted along its torso and neck, an orchard of purplish flesh.

"Just one," the man said, "Bring it to me and we will let you eat with those that have sent them. You can't understand joy, until ..."

But the man's final words were cut off by a hollow crunch, the sound of splitting wood. There was a groan, then something colliding with the stone step, wet and hollow. I couldn't turn away from the creature. It stared out with a single mournful eye, the globes growing from its body hanging about its ruined face. There was a hand on my shoulder, an arm around my waist, Cashel screaming in my ear, Mark swearing as he tried to uproot my feet while I reached forward, toward the creature, the man's promise singing in my ear as my mouth grew wet.

Cashel and Mark managed to tip me backward, to drag me by the shoulders through the doorway, over the body of the man, a broken skateboard lying beside him, blood on the grip tape, crimson splotches marring the snow. My eyes were drawn to the sky, to the thousands of pinpricks disrupting the blackness, the distance, the ones who accepted the offered fruit. My heels dragged through the damp accumulation, across concrete, until they jammed me in the backseat of Cashel's car, upholstery reeking of weed and French fries. The roof over my head was singed with burns from cigarettes ashed over a shoulder with the window open, a thousand black suns.

"Maybe night wasn't the best option," Cashel said.

"I don't think daytime would be any better," Mark replied from the seat beside me, hands pressed to my chest, pinning me.

"Guys. It's fine. Just let me out. It will be like one second," my mouth worked faster than my thoughts. "They just want the fruit. It's just fruit."

"Nope," Cashel said, slamming the door. He jumped into the driver's seat and engaged the childproof locks. I tried the handle, but it wouldn't budge. Mark slapped my hand away from the cool metal. "We've still got nine songs to finish."

"And neither one of us wants to sing vocals," Mark said.

Cashel sped off the front lawn where he'd parked, skidding through the snow, tearing up grass, bumper dropping low as he careened over the curb. Through the rear window, through the red-stained glass, the starscape hung, a black smear above the altar. None of those gathered turned at the sound of screeching tires, at the metal grind of steel sliding over curb. Only the mournful hum from the shed, louder than anything I'd ever heard, dragged them from their prayers as we pulled right on Route 28. A low E wavered through the air, calling them to their next harvest.

It was distinct, undeniable.

Maybe I wasn't tone deaf after all.

Maybe I'd just never really listened.

■

Corey Farrenkopf lives on Cape Cod with his wife, Gabrielle, and works as a librarian. His short stories have been published in Three-Lobed Burning Eye, Vastarien, Smokelong Quarterly, Uncharted, Catapult, The Southwest Review, Reckoning, Flash Fiction Online, *and elsewhere. To learn more, follow him on twitter @CoreyFarrenkopf or on the web at CoreyFarrenkopf.com*

THE RIGHT TIME

■

Nico Montoya

She'd reminded us that we were ab-so-lutely not permitted any flash photography inside. None. Did we understand?

Standing at attention, side by side in the sand, we had kept our eyes on the horizon, as we'd been trained.

She'd paced, pausing briefly in front of each of us to take an incredulous peek through the so-called windows to our souls. For some, she'd tugged at our beards or earlobes in this or that direction so she could get a better angle for this routine character assessment.

So. Did we—turn your head this way—understand or—hmm—not?

We had, one-by-one, answered that, yes, we understood Her Holiness.

Good. Because anachronists, she'd said, gesticulating histrionically, anachronists have no place here anymore. Right?

Right, we'd told Her Holiness. Right, right, right. Of course not.

Certainly not in her own staff.

Of course not, Your Holiness.

They'd be ready for the first prisoner, she'd said, an hour after dinner exactly. Exactly, she'd repeated. Would we be there on time? She would not be back out here to remind us.

Yes, we'd told Her Holiness. Nothing matters more than being at the right place at the right time.

We'd said this in unison, with conviction, as we'd been trained.

This is a big day for me, she'd said.

We know.

So don't fuck it up.

We won't.

After a final scan, skeptical, she'd then turned and gone into the temple for her Boozy Brunch with the Pharaoh and his retinue.

Nothing matters more than being at the right place at the right time.

· · ·

We'd waited outside, in the creeping shadow of the temple. Through the brunch, and whatever debauchery came after brunch, and the preparations for dinner, and all that. Waiting, waiting, waiting.

The prisoner was delivered to us by chariot as the sun set. It was an unusually beautiful sunset. We quickly, secretly snapped a couple pics of it, but we couldn't capture the bigness of it on that little screen.

The prisoner had graying ginger braids, blue face paint, and a wooly green and gray tartan outfit thing with a miscellany of metal and leather adornments and affordances here and there. She was badly sunburned and stank like hell. Some of her teeth were missing. Great muscle definition on those arms though. Especially for someone her age. We agreed she must have been from the British Isles. Some of us argued Late Antiquity, others the Early Middle Ages. We tried to ask her. She spat and said something rude-sounding, but we weren't familiar with her language.

The charioteer handed us the other end of our new prisoner's leash, gave her a sonorous spank and laughed as she tripped out of the chariot. Welp, getting dark, he said, slapping his dusty hands on his dusty knees. Wished he could stay, but needed to get back to the city and all that. About an hour drive, you know. Don't give her too much slack, okay? She's a crafty one.

The prisoner, one of us asked. Or the High Priestess?

We all had a good laugh about that.

The charioteer shrugged and smiled clownishly before taking off.

The prisoner spat again. We pulled the rope a little tighter. It was tied around her wrists, which were looking pretty raw, but she didn't wince. Just glared.

It was still a few minutes until the hearing, so we had some time to kill.

We looked around. No potential witnesses. One of us took out an iPhone, we snapped a quick selfie with our scowling pet barbarian.

How did it turn out? How did it turn out? How did it—

We huddled around the phone to see if we were each at our most photogenic.

The pic was blurry in the waning sunlight. Need to hold everything stiller when it's a longer exposure like that. And one of us had blinked anyway. And it was all off-center and crooked. Amateur hour. Come on.

We started to pose for a second take, but a burly pharaonic guard with a glinting khopesh in his belt stumbled out of the temple. We hid the phone, acted natural, gave him a salute. He gave us a nod, and then he turned, rearranged the front of his garments, pissed on the foundation for what must have been a minute and a half, and then finally zigzagged back inside.

Now it's time to bring the prisoner before her judges.

Nothing matters more than being at the right place at the right time.

We stash our phones in a little leather drawstring pouch, with some other supplies, in the only tent left in the camp. The sun is down now.

This is our first time inside. We'd be lying if we said we're not stoked.

In the dimness, the interior seems colored by a palate modeled on dying coals, deep grays accented with glowing reds. It takes our pupils a second to dilate and refocus in the comparative darkness, but soon we're able to behold the immensity from inside.

We're sad we can't take a picture of it, but a picture wouldn't capture the bigness anyway.

The flap, flop, flap, flop of our sandy sandals echoes in the immense hall. We march in 2/4 time through the eternal colonnade, allegro staccato, 120 bpm. Flap, flop, flap, flop. We tug our prisoner along. Her pendulous red-gray braids tick tock as we march.

On either side of us, every column is a unique anthropomorphic colossus. Unique in that they are all standing with somewhat different poses. They're all males though. No, we can't see sandstone beards or anything like that way up there in the blackness, where the roof must yoke their unmoving heads. Heads that might be the head of a jackal, an ibis, a crocodile, a bull, a falcon, a man. Who knows? It's too dark at that altitude so far above us. But we can see up their over-starched skirts a little, because beside each figure is a tripod, and each tripod holds a huge earthenware bowl, and each bowl holds a pool of date palm oil, and each pool of oil holds a red and blue flame. The light from the flames burbles up the sandstone calves of the colossi as we move between those two longer-than-a-city-block rows of them. And—arriving at the point—even up in the fading radius of firelight we can see that the imperial sculptors left little uncertainty as to whether these big stony fellas were also colossally hung.

Flap, flop, flap, flop.

We walk abreast, contemplating the capriciousness of the gods with regard to our own varied genital endowments. Two of us have the prisoner by the elbows. Her chin is high and she is not resisting. Physically, that is. Her lack of resistance is itself a form of defiance, saying I come here of my own choosing, and not by your imperative. Which, although cute, is untrue.

The sweet and spicy smoke of myrrh grows more pungent as we approach a large golden platform at the far back. Upon it are more fiery tripods and a plastic craft services table with some wine, crudité, charcuterie, chips, guac, hummus, salsa.

Lounging at floor-level in the wings are the guards and wives and concubines and exotic menagerie. Peacocks, baboons, kudus, cheetahs. All with bejeweled collars.

Elevated and slightly off-center stands Her Holiness, the High Priestess. She's in her impossibly white linen, as always. It's like a kind of pantsuit or romper or something. Her signature look. It says both business and leisure. It transitions seamlessly from day to night. It's expensive. Very expensive. She often reminds us of this when we're getting too close to her with our grubby hands.

She looks out at us, steady and impassive. Without moving her neck, she pours a sensible quantity of wine from a small bowl into her mouth. Head straight and level, she looks down at us with only her eyes as we come nearer to the foot of the high platform. Beside her, centered, and in a lion-footed throne, the Pharaoh slouches in standard Old Kingdom pharaonic regalia, appearing distracted and irritated as he jabs with his thumbs at the keys of his Blackberry.

Flap, flop, flap, flop.

Halt.

The High Priestess is holding out her palm toward us. The universal, unichronal stop sign.

The Pharaoh continues to thumb the keys of his device. Click, click, clickclickclick.

Click, click.

Click.

We glance at each other and back at the High Priestess, thinking like so, we'll just wait for His Majesty to finish sending his royal email then, or ...?

But the Pharaoh eventually grumbles something, sets his Blackberry down on the arm of his throne, and looks up. The High Priestess metamorphoses her stop sign hand into a down arrow. We genuflect and lower our gazes, precisely as she's trained us.

The prisoner continues to stand and look up at her assessors, defiant in her woolen garments, practically rags. One of us tugs her down to one knee with the rest of us.

Ouch, fuck, she whispers.

Oh, so now she speaks our language, huh?

Hail! Hail His Majesty the Pharaoh! We shout this as one, just as we've been trained.

Jesus Christ, he says, I'm right in front of you.

We look up to see him grimace and Q-tip his ear with his pinky. The High Priestess is giving us a reprimanding look, like we hadn't done exactly as she'd trained us?

Hey, uh, the Pharaoh says to the High Priestess. Top me off? Please and thank you.

He holds out a small empty bowl to her. Of course, she says as she sets down her own bowl on the craft services table, and from a golden vase she fills His Majesty's vessel to the brim with dark Phoenician wine.

Thanks, sweetheart, cheers, he says as he takes it from her, with a little nod and an emphatic toasting motion in her direction. Oh, shit, sorry.

He'd splashed some onto her until-then impossibly white expensive linen pantsuit romper outfit thing.

Jesus, I'm so sorry, I—

It's nothing, Your Majesty. She smiles like an air stewardess and then grabs a paper napkin from the plastic table, tries to dab up the stain, still smiling obsequiously.

The Pharaoh tries to help: Here, let me—

No, no, she says. It's fine, I got most of... It's fine. There. See? See?

She pinches out the damp front of her still empurpled vestments for him to assess.

The Pharaoh raises an eyebrow and looks back at us.

Your boss is really the independent type, eh?

He laughs and we can tell we're supposed to laugh too, so we do, and we try not to sound nervous about this little betrayal of our entrepreneurial supervisor.

The prisoner laughs along with us, but does this much louder sarcastic laugh, really dripping with unflinching defiance. It echoes impressively. Ha! Ha! Ha! (Ha, ha, ha, ha...)

So, are we going to do this, says the Pharaoh, checking a notification on his Blackberry, setting it back down, then taking a drink of his wine.

The High Priestess clears her throat, faces the prisoner.

You stand before the altar of Tempor, she says. The new god. The old god. The god of timeliness, the god of punctuality. He who is, who was, and who will be.

Her words bounce through the enormous dark chamber.

The prisoner sucks her teeth, nonplussed.

You stand accused, says the Priestess, of being in the wrong place at the wrong time.

The prisoner spits.

The High Priestess clenches her fists and then relaxes them.

State your name, she says.

Go fuck yourself.

One of us whaps the prisoner in the back of the head with an open palm. She snarls and snaps her teeth like a big ugly crocodile.

The Pharaoh shakes his head and starts multitasking on his Blackberry again.

Prisoner, says Her Holiness, I advise you to cooperate.

I advise you to cooperate, says the prisoner in a pitch-perfect parroting. Ha! Ha! Ha! (Ha, ha, ha, ha...)

We try not to laugh too. The impression is spot on. The nasal intonation, the arched eyebrows, everything.

The Pharaoh chuckles a little, puts his phone back down.

Bring her up here, he says.

...

Her Holiness tells Pharaoh that she doesn't really think that's such a good—

Shush, says Pharoah. Up here. Come on.

We look at each other.

You can cut her out of that, uh, that ropy thing first, he says, pointing at the ropy thing around her wrists.

We look to Her Holiness, who shrugs, exasperation in her eyes.

We look at each other again, like: who's even got a knife though?

Some of us have concealed Leatherman multi-tools, true, but those are technically anachronistic contraband. No way we're taking those out in here right now, of all times and places. Nothing is more important than being in the right place at the right time, and yadda, yadda, yadda.

The drunk guard from earlier is standing in the wings, and he goes, I got you, fam, and he struts up with his khopesh. Flap, flop, flap, flop.

Thanks, man, we say.

He presses and saws and slices the prisoner free but, oops, gives her a big gash on her wrist as the rope finally surrenders to his blade all at once.

Shit, shit, shit, shit, sorry, he says. Shit, I—

There's blood everywhere. Practically spraying. There's gasping and murmuring and commotion in the wings. It's a whole thing.

We look at each other again like, uh, shit, what do we do?

The prisoner rips off some of her raggedy skirt and wraps it around the wound, pulling it tight with the non-bleeding hand and her teeth.

The High Priestess closes her eyes, rubs her temples, seems to be working hard to keep her breathing steady.

We ask her if she could hand us some of those paper napkins from over there on the table, please? Or ...

She sighs, passes down a handful of them. We use them to soak up as much as we can. The napkins become heavy with warm blood and start to tear and fall apart as we scrub them over the rough floor.

The Pharaoh looks impatient.

Everyone good now? Yeah?

We don't know what to do with the bloody napkins so we kind of just stuff them in our pockets.

Yeah, we say. Yeah, we're good.

Okay, says the Pharaoh. Up she goes then. Come on.

The platform is a solid three or four cubits off the ground with no stairs that we can see. We walk the prisoner to it and a couple of us hoist her up. It's not graceful. She's heavier than she looks. She kind of flops on her face and her skirt comes up. She must have lost a couple pints of blood and looks woozy.

But she pulls herself upright nevertheless, adjusts her rags, and stands tall before His Majesty, the Pharaoh.

Jesus Christ, says the Pharaoh, averting his nose. You couldn't bathe her before this?

Sorry, we say. We—

The Pharaoh shushes us with his hand.

Prisoner, he says. Are you an anachronist?

I don't know what that means.

Is this when you belong?

I fucking hope not. Ha! Ha! Ha! (Ha, ha, ha, ha...)

He waits for the echo to finish.

How did you end up here and now, he says.

How? Well. So, this handsy little dipshit with a chariot—

Your majesty, the High Priestess interrupts. The prisoner was arrested in the—

Hey, says the Pharaoh. Hey. Shush. Both of you. I haven't got the energy for this kind of—

• • •

Her Holiness begins to apologize.

At the same time, off in the wings, a tethered baboon steals a concubine's paper plate of pears and pomegranate seeds and honeydew and retreats to the corner. The audacious primate tries to gobble it all up before he can be discovered and reeled in and disfrugivated. But it's all in vain. He's noticed immediately and he screams as his prize is snatched away by his embarrassed handlers.

The commotion is loud and draws everyone's attention.

The prisoner uses the distraction to attempt her escape.

She takes off her shoe and uses it to slap the High Priestess across the cheek. Whap. She then pushes Her Holiness into the craft services table, toppling both into a pile of meats and cheeses and vegetables and a rainbow of salty dips. Then the prisoner pushes over one of the flaming tripods and, as the burning oil spills and makes a fiery smear across the stage, she jumps down and starts running back for the front doors of the temple. With what plan once she's outside? We couldn't begin to guess.

We just stand there, kind of dumbstruck by the whole situation.

The prisoner is really legging it, hobbled only a bit by having only one shoe on.

Some concubines have already put out most of the fire with a tablecloth and they're checking on the High Priestess. She's okay, she's fine, thank you, she's fine.

The prisoner is halfway along the colonnade, shrinking away in the distance, her footsteps echoing as she books it the hell out of there.

The Pharaoh turns to the guards in charge of the cheetahs. He hesitates, blankets his face in his hands for a second, but finally gives them a disappointed thumbs up. They nod.

The cheetahs had already been tracking the prisoner, crouching low, waggling their rumps, pulling at their leads.

The guards release them.

Zoom.

Their paws are soft on the temple floor.

They'll be on the prisoner in a flash.

She'll never even know she was being chased until she's pinned to the ground with those sharp teeth in her neck. And then her days of anachronizing will be over.

Thus to those in the wrong place at the wrong time.

. . .

We'll come back in the morning to clean, after Pharoah and his people have packed up and made the trek back to the palace. The little fire bowls will have run through their fuel, but the sun will be slipping through slits high on the walls and we'll be able to see everything a lot better. Turns out it's actually pretty colorful inside. Blues and golds and blacks and whites and reds. And, sure, it'll all still look enormous, but it won't feel as infinite as it did in the dark, when we couldn't even see all the way up to the ceiling.

Turns out the columnal colossi will have human heads after all. All identical, as far as we can tell from down here.

Her Holiness will be recuperating in her personal chamber behind the altar. The door will be closed. She will have told us that she is ab-so-lutely not to be disturbed this morning under any circumstances whatsoever, do we understand?

We'll be wheeling around a plastic yellow janitorial rig that holds a mop and bucket and paper towels and various acerbic chemicals. But before we start to scrub at the animal droppings and food and blood and the burn marks on the high platform and gods know what else, we'll look over our shoulders and, when we know the coast is clear, we'll snap a few quick photos.

■

Nico Montoya writes fiction in Northeast Minneapolis, where he lives with one wife, two kids, and three cats. You can find some of his other speculative stories in journals such as Pembroke Magazine, X-R-A-Y, *and* Apple Valley Review. *Find him on the platform formerly known as Twitter @NicoMontoya89.*

BEACH DAY

■

Shane Inman

Buddy and I drove to the park near my apartment first because I liked the kids who lived around there the best. Down-to-earth sorts I could picture driving an ice cream truck like mine one day, or maybe building castles like my great-grandfather. Negotiations with their parents began while I was still a few blocks away, the moment they heard that tin-can jingle. Just one, just enough for one, please, just the one, and I promise I won't ask for anything else all week. You know, savvy kids. The kind whose folks didn't turn me into a cautionary tale the moment I was out of earshot, a bogeyman intended to keep straight-A report cards coming in. I liked the way these kids watched me with a sort of awe, as if owning a truck full of ice cream was a greater aspiration than becoming an astronaut.

When they looked at me that way, I felt like I really *did* own the truck and didn't have to worry about the rising tide of those increasingly aggressive letters piling up on my kitchen table.

The park wasn't much to look at—a triangle of fume-wilted grass stretched between the road to the docks and the road to the waste transfer facility. Creaky basketball hoops hunched over a rectangle of broken blacktop, but the court was totally empty. It was already a very hot day. Across from the hoops a couple dozen kids huddled under the shade of a single maple that had long ago caught whatever disease maples catch and never grew leaves on its eastern side, even during the summer. I don't think it was dying, but it wasn't not dying either. Just sort of holding on, snatching up whatever scraps of photosynthetic currency it could find in the latter hours of the day and using those not to grow or heal but simply to remain. It probably needed a companion tree to shield it from the world's harsher currents, but I'm not a treeologist, so what do I know.

Anyway, like I said, the kids knew I was coming and had already squeezed whatever coins and crumpled bills they could from reluctant parents. About half rushed toward me as I pulled up to the curb, while the other half either ratcheted up their pleas and pulled out all the stops or kicked forlornly at the dirt because their parents were at work and they had nobody to ask in the first place. I'll admit that as much as I liked these kids, I always felt a little tug of guilt about coming here. A day at the park was free. That was basically the whole point. Maybe you bring a couple sandwiches and a bottle of water, but otherwise you could mark it down on your budget as a big ol' zero. My presence changed that, a fact written all too clearly on the faces of a few moms and dads, pleased that their child was pleased but already doing calculations about how that money might have been better spent. But that's just how it goes. I didn't have the breathing room to get all tangled up about it.

"Hi." A real skinny kid had been the first to reach the truck and he wasn't even out of breath. Little champion, that one.

"Morning," I said. "What'll it be, sir?"

He counted the quarters in his hand, scrunched his lips against his cheek, and pointed. "Rocket Pop, please."

"Original or cherry?"

"Regular."

"Coming right up."

I took his coins, tossed them into the cash drawer, and went to fetch his popsicle from the freezer. I had to push Buddy aside because he was lying right on the plastic packets I needed, rigid as anything. It was probably a health code violation of some kind, but I figured he couldn't do any harm while he was frozen, and besides I couldn't leave him out in the heat all day. God, can you imagine? So I fished out the popsicle and handed it to the kid and sent him off happy as can be and took my next diminutive customer's order.

I launched a lot of Rocket Pops there. American classics, multicolored missiles which dye lips red and white before concluding with a tasteful asphyxiation blue. A few ice cream sandwiches and orange Dreamsicles went too, but none of the kids sprang for the big-ticket items, the cartoon character pops or the Choco Tacos. When the last customer ambled away, vanilla droplets plopping onto his T-shirt, I counted my meager earnings. I could already hear the water sloshing against my truck, rising fast, waiting for one good riptide to yank the whole thing away from me. I'd have to hit the shore today, no two ways about it.

As I left, I almost stopped for this one kid who hadn't succeeded in securing any capital. He was so pitiful, mopey and breathing too hard—probably asthma, like lots of kids around here have—and I nearly handed him a free popsicle just for the trouble of being alive. I really did want to.

· · ·

Buddy was a cat, before you get the wrong idea. I didn't have a dead man in my freezer. Just a dead cat called Buddy, named after my city's most beloved felon. I don't know exactly how old he was, having found him meowing and mean-looking outside my apartment one drizzly Tuesday, but I kept him for almost fifteen years and he was the closest thing I had to anything. Buddy was never an affectionate cat, not one of those who snakes around your arms while you're reading and covers you in hair and little trills. But he always let me know he was around. I'd get home from another long day, back all fucked up from hunching over the freezer for hours, and he wouldn't greet me, exactly, but I could see the shimmer of his eyes watching from the next room, where he'd stay just long enough to reassure me I wasn't alone before he disappeared again into whatever space he existed in most of the time. So when I found him—a week or so before the very hot day—stiff on his side under my bed, I didn't know what to do. I didn't have time to take him anywhere and I didn't actually know what one was supposed to do with a dead pet so I put him in the freezer and decided I'd deal with him later. But at the end of the day I was so tired, and looking at the little tortoiseshell body in my freezer only added to my exhaustion, so I left him there and told myself I'd give him a proper burial the next day, or the next. Except I'd need to do research on what a proper burial looked like for an animal. The last thing I wanted was to do it wrong, after Buddy had been so good to me. And I didn't have a yard, which posed another problem. You might be thinking cremation, but I didn't think he would want to be erased like that. No, whatever I was going to do, it was going to take a long time to figure out. In the meantime I could just keep him frozen, looking more or less like he did in life. Sometimes at night I'd crack open the freezer and stroke him behind his rock-solid ear—just for a moment and only with one finger to avoid any chance of a thaw.

So he'd still been in the freezer on the morning of the very hot day when I decided to put him in my truck instead. My landlord had been threatening to kick me out for the past couple weeks, and I had a feeling this time he really meant it. I didn't want to come home to see Buddy discarded on the sidewalk with all my belongings and being devoured by hungry carnivores. Here I could protect him from that, just like he'd always protected me from how still everything got at night. It was actually kind of nice, knowing he was right there with me as I lurched onto the highway. I'd never taken Buddy on the job before, scared he might leap out the window someplace far from home and I'd never see him again. But he was safe now. It was just the two of us and he wasn't going anywhere.

You only have to go so far south on a hot Sunday before the highway really starts to clot. Brake lights congealing, flow halting, pressure spiking. Every minute I spent idling was another minute's worth of gas money I'd never get back and another minute of losing sales to a rival driver. I was getting pretty antsy by the half-hour mark, but at least I had company, even if he was in the back and couldn't speak English and was also dead.

"You seeing this guy?" I said, loud enough to be heard through the freezer's heavy lid. I nodded toward a gleaming black Mercedes with a Coexist bumper sticker. "What an asshole. I hope someone steals his car."

Nobody would, but it was nice to dream.

As I continued south, the composition of the traffic changed. Hondas and Fords and Toyotas made way for Cadillacs, BMWs, and the occasional Tesla operating on autopilot while a white-haired white guy in a white button-down folded his hands behind his head and stretched his legs, his right foot nowhere near the brake pedal—trusting not so much the machine itself as the status it conveyed. As I willed those lithium batteries to combust in the way they often liked to do, I realized the traffic might have been getting to me more than I'd anticipated.

Well, fuck it. I muscled my way over a couple lanes and took the next exit. I wasn't even sure where it led but the sign said Beach Access so it seemed as good an option as any. What waited for me was the most lifeless beach I'd ever seen. It met the minimum requirements—there was the sand, there was the water—and aspired to nothing else. Still, a small crowd had set up blankets and umbrellas and parking was plentiful so I flipped on the jingle and found a good spot by the curb. The people my tinny song drew in were, like the beach they'd chosen for their sweltering leisure day, thoroughly ordinary. Paper people. That guy there was probably a middle manager in a nearby office park. The woman after him had almost certainly dedicated her life to a mildly successful hair salon a few miles inland. This kid likely had a dog named Spot or Sparky. The couple next in line stood neither too close nor too far apart but maintained that just-right distance of people who aren't exactly in love anymore but, you know, also don't hate each other yet. It was like everyone had been drained of something. Or had given it up willingly in exchange for something else. I handed over cold crinkly packages and dropped coins and bills into the register.

The line dwindled and I was about to call it quits on that place when I saw an old woman lying face down in the sand. Not on a towel or under an umbrella but sprawled there like she'd fallen and simply accepted her fate.

She could've been someone's grandmother but neither children nor grandchildren appeared to check on her. I pointed while handing my last customer a Drumstick.

"She okay?"

"Oh." He shaded his eyes and looked her over. "No, I don't think so. It's too hot for some folks."

I was about to ask him if someone ought to help but he, uninterested in the conversation, wandered back to his family, staring fixedly at the Drumstick wrapper as he wrestled it open. I wanted to help the lady. Honest. But the longer I stayed there the worse the traffic was going to get, and I really needed to reach the islands if I hoped to so much as break even. I took a quarter from the drawer and pelted it at the motionless form. I don't know why I did that except that it was the only thing I could think to do for her. I'm a pretty good thrower and the coin bounced off her head and landed in the blazing sand beside her. She didn't move. I turned off the jingle and left.

I had to crank the A/C up all the way by the time I reached the big suspension bridge, something I really try not to do on account of that extra gas usage and the fact that everything eventually fails if pushed too hard for too long. But the heat was too thick, like the sun was boiling over and all that hot foam had settled on top of us. It wasn't even noon. Atop the bridge's tower, where the great sweeping arms of cable intersected, a man was suspended horizontally by a harness, feet braced against the tower and shoulders hovering over nothing. He sprayed something across the metal surface, added slack to his harness, and took a step backward toward the sea.

"Do you think I could do a job like that?" I asked Buddy. "You'd catch me if I slipped, wouldn't you?"

The thing about the biggest island is that it's full of castles and people actually live in them. Technically they're called cottages, but I know a castle when I see one—seventy rooms overlooking a sprawling rose garden which itself overlooks a two-hundred-foot drop to the foaming waves. Eventually those waves will eat so much of the rock face that the rose garden and the mansion will tumble into the surf, but I'll be long dead by then and there'll be no one to go to my grave and say hey, guess what just fucking happened. Buddy might've done it if he'd outlived me. Ah, well.

These castles are also why the island is the best place to set up on a very hot day. If I could track down the kings or dukes or whatever they called themselves, I'd be set. Those people would buy anything in any quantity and I could even charge extra without them noticing. No price was too high.

I never felt bad about overcharging those assholes because my great-grandfather built one of their castles, or so I'm told. My grandmother told me he worked a night shift, slathering mortar and hauling immense pillars by lantern light because a Vanderbilt's brother had just completed the most expensive mansion on the bluffs—a work of art chiseled from blocks of Italian marble heavy enough to kill—and that simply wouldn't do. So the Vanderbilt sent word from New York that his own mansion needed to be even bigger and needed to be completed faster than humanly possible or else he'd be struck from The Mrs. Astor's party roster and his entire life would be *ruined*.

Each time I glimpse that castle I see not the finished product (marvel though it is) but a skeletal thing bathed in the uncertain light of gas lamps like some Roman ruin uncovered by 19th century archaeologists. And there, atop the unfinished walls, stands my great-grandfather. Except he died as a young man so he's never more than a silhouette, too dark to see.

The A/C started grumbling after we crossed the bridge and I pleaded with it to hold on for one more day, though I actually needed it to hold on forever because where the hell was I going to get a spare fifteen hundred dollars for a new compressor? Just the thought of it choked me, saltwater pooling in my lungs. I punched the dash once, twice, three times, and I must've made a pretty good case for myself because it kept on chugging as we made for the island's biggest beach.

God that place was packed. Fucking unbelievably so. Bumper to bumper two miles out, nearly a standstill closer in. The sign outside a Citizens Bank branch cheerily declared the temperature had broken 100 degrees. All I could do was sit there, sweating, losing money I didn't have.

"You okay back there, Bud?" I said over my shoulder.

He didn't answer, but that was just par for the course with him. A real contrary cat. You couldn't so much as hint at what you wanted from him or else he'd do the opposite. After a while I learned not to look for Buddy when I needed him. When I'd come home early that spring with a cardboard box full of my mother, I just sat at the kitchen table and stared at the dark and didn't move and after a long time Buddy came and lay down in the far corner of the room. His eyes glimmered in the shadows like they knew me. There was no comfort there, exactly, but it made me feel like I had someone.

My mother used to tell me there was no secret to life. No answer to the questions it posed. You just had to put your head down and bear all the trouble it heaped on you and count yourself lucky if you had somebody by your side when the heat became too much and you melted into a sticky puddle of goo. She told me this a lot, a mantra she repeated more for her own benefit than mine. But I was working when she got sick and working when the sick got her so I wasn't by her side at all, just like she wasn't there for her own parents and no one was there for my great-grandfather. I guess that's why I never bothered with a family of my own. We're just not lucky like that. Though if my great-grandfather, sweat-drenched, asks me on my deathbed why the line is ending, why all his labor has amounted to nothing, I'm not sure I'll be able to give him a satisfactory answer. I had a cat, I'll tell him. A cat who cared whether I lived or died.

I finally reached the beach parking just as the attendant put out a "Lot Full" sign. An F-350 snapped it in half and drove right in but the attendant didn't seem too fazed and just got a new sign from his booth and put that one out instead, then watched as another big, muscly car bowled that one over too while the kids in the back seats fought over some device and their parents threatened to take everything from them. These people were going to have their fucking relaxing beach day even if they had to kill someone for it. They had put in their time, they had sold off their best years, and now this—this one annihilatingly hot day—was what they were owed, and no one would take it from them. I'll admit I was a little jealous of those red, shouting families. They were so unhappy, but they were other things too.

I blew past the attendant like the others. He'd probably lose his job, but I couldn't worry about that right then. I'd taken too long in getting there and the beachside curb was already lined with my competitors, folks just like me who I felt intensely violent toward in that moment. Whatever goodwill I'd felt at the park in the city had by then entirely evaporated, joining the thick oceanic haze where all the good of society went when it got too hot out. I screeched into an illegal spot on the sidewalk behind the other trucks and threw on my jingle. Every truck blared its music at full volume. All together, it sounded like Hades. None of the kids in line seemed remotely bothered and I kind of resented them for that. They were so oblivious to this awful thing that the rest of us had to deal with. Those at the back of the existing queues dashed over to me to cut short that excruciating period between wanting something and receiving it. Some of them even bought the Banana Bars, so they must've been pretty desperate.

I started to realize something was wrong as I handed a Dora the Explorer pop to some giddy six-year-old. I felt it first as a bead sliding down the groove beside my right nostril. It meandered along the bow above my upper lip then dripped and landed noiselessly on the truck's sill.

"Hot one, isn't it?" said a dad-aged dad as he flicked open his wallet.

"Sure is," I said. It was the third time I'd had this exchange in the last ten minutes, but the words actually meant something this time. Because it was a hot one. God it was a hot one. I waved a hand over the dashboard vents and felt only hot air. Something inside had broken. That explained why the freezer was chugging louder than usual, struggling pitifully against that giant fusion engine in the sky. I stroked Buddy's ear and his fur was soft and damp, slowly thawing. I poked a Rocket Pop and it gave just a little. Inside that wrapper it must have been bleeding all over itself, red white and blue dissolving into a sticky disgusting mess. If I didn't offload all this shit before it melted, I'd end the day so far in the red I'd drown in it. Forget the compressor, I'd lose the whole damn truck. The apartment. The only things besides my dear dead cat I could still call my own. But there was no way I'd sell everything that quick. Not here, not with all those other trucks lined up in front of me. I needed to outsmart the market.

I abandoned the families in my line, hopped into the driver's seat, and threw the truck into drive. The main road was still backed up all to shit and it looked like there'd just been an accident in the parking lot, because two women were punching the hell out of each other while their husbands and kids cheered them on. No getting out that way. So I just edged the rest of the way off the curb in the other direction, onto the sand, asking Buddy to cross his toes and pray the wheels wouldn't stick.

It's easy enough once you get the hang of it. Driving on sand, I mean. It's not too different from driving on snow. You go a little slower than usual, try not to turn too sharply, and do your best to ignore the expletives hurled by people diving out of your way. It wasn't that I enjoyed plowing through picnics and snapping umbrellas and popping big inflatable balls—I just didn't have the luxury of caring at that particular moment. I swear I'm not a callous person.

Eventually the crowds thinned out and then disappeared behind me and the drive was pretty nice after that. Just the ocean on my left and shiny wet sand stretching out in front of me. Sort of romantic except for how sweaty I was getting. That part was really gross. I kept punching the dashboard but nothing came out, even as bloody cuts opened on my knuckles. I yelled some really nasty stuff at the truck and apologized to Buddy for my language and then yelled some more.

By the time I got to where I was going, I must've looked like an absolute wreck, because when the security SUV stopped me the guy inside already had a hand on his gun.

"You can't be here," he said, stepping out of the car with his fingers wrapped around the pistol grip. Big beefy guy, neck like a tree trunk. I thought I recognized him from my own neighborhood. "This is a private beach."

Past him, people stared. Pale, stylishly dressed, sun hats all over the place. I swear to god some of them were playing croquet on the sand.

"Oh, I didn't know," I said, even though I did.

"You're gonna have to pay."

I squinted up at the bluffs, and there they were, the castles. I had this feeling they were watching me. They didn't know who I was, couldn't feel my great-grandfather's bones fertilizing their gardens. They just knew I didn't belong. Which was weird, because it wasn't like this was a different beach than the one I'd just left. It was all the same coast.

"There's been a misunderstanding," I said. "I have ice cream. I'm here to sell ice cream."

"Oh," the guard said, and for the first time seemed to register the bright colors of the menu plastered on my truck. He let go of his gun. "I'll have a Big Dipper."

It's that easy sometimes. You just need something to offer.

Pretty soon, a whole crowd had gathered around me and I was handing out every sort of treat I had. For the first time since that morning it started to feel like a good day. Maybe it would all work out. No one ever said "keep the change" but it was all right because I upcharged them outrageously. And god, those kids were hungry. Like I've never seen. Some would buy an ice cream sandwich, devour it in front of me, then order another. I didn't know how the hell they got so ravenous, but I wasn't about to stop serving them. It did start to make me uneasy though, the way they never seemed to fill up, kept coming back for more even as my supply dwindled. I looked to their parents for some sort of backup but the adults had gotten over their initial shock at my intrusion and returned to their natural state of being unable to register my existence.

Very slowly, I handed out the last crinkly package I had. A dozen kids waited expectantly for more.

"That's all I have," I said. "Sorry."

They begged, then, and when that didn't work they started demanding. I told them I'd be back tomorrow but they weren't having it. A couple of them stood in front of the truck so I couldn't leave.

"More," they said. "More."

I went to the freezer to double check. Nothing. Only Buddy.

The security guard came up to me and said, in a low voice, that I'd better give them what they wanted. Said they were still hungry.

I spread my hands and told him I had nothing left except for one thing which wasn't for sale.

"Give them that, then."

"I can't. He's mine." Sweat rivered down my back. The gas needle inched closer to E. I opened the cash drawer and did a quick count and came up with Not Enough. Even after all this I was going to sink because of course I was—I'd been too far out to sea long before the day began. How had I managed to convince myself otherwise?

And there were those kids, innocent little fuckers, all-American grins and outstretched dollar bills and the beginnings of sunburns blooming on their necks.

"It's very expensive," I said. I had to say it twice because the first time the words just sort of croaked out and didn't sound like words at all. The kids ran back to their parents and returned with more money, held tight in their fists so the sea breeze wouldn't steal it. I could already feel how still my apartment would be once I returned, how loud every step would become with no one left to hear it.

I took the money. Put it in the drawer one bill at a time, counting them. How much is anything worth, really? Then I pulled Buddy from the freezer. I meant to say something to him, some kind of meaningful goodbye, but the next thing I knew I was handing him over and I hadn't said even one word. The kids cheered. They grabbed Buddy's legs, his tail, his head. With a little effort they pulled him limb from limb. Decapitated him. Wrenched his spine in two. I stood there and watched them dig their little canines into his frozen tendons, slurp at dangling arteries, crunch down on exposed ribs and gnaw chunks of yellow fat with glee. Their lips and teeth turned Rocket Pop red. The melting juices dribbled down their chins and onto their chests and little dots of it speckled the sand.

Past them the water sparkled under the sun. Gentle waves repeated themselves. I thought about what it all must look like from the castle on the bluffs that my great-grandfather built. I bet it looks so pretty.

■

Shane Inman's work appears in The Forge, Mud Season Review, Vol. 1 Brooklyn, Stoneboat, *and elsewhere. He received his MFA in the southwest and lives in Philadelphia.*

COVER ART

ON VA FLUNCHER

———————— ■ ————————

arnus

Ugly since 1982, the artist arnus is quite a joke.

He does not hesitate to grind and mix personal and pop culture stories, to bring out mischievous and terrifying characters like schoolchildren who have learned their lessons badly...

Don't get me wrong, they are, of course, sometimes unsightly and repulsive, but, lurking in the guise of a smiling demon, a good joke is never far from bursting... And then there's color anyway, damn it!

A fan of experimental rock, he started in the early 2000s as an illustrator for concert posters, then found himself invited to participate in various international works for the vast world of micro-publishing.

We find his work here and there, in the bends of an alley in Latvia, on the cover of a Komikaze in Croatia, on the door of a squat in Berlin, on the door of an elevator in Nice (well, almost, his fresco has just been sanded by the new owner of the place) or in some fanzines and artbooks such as Hey! artbook or on the Hi-Fructose website.

He exhibits regularly wherever we want him, in France, even in Europe, and says hello to you.

THANK YOU!

PATREON SUPPORTERS:

Jer Blane

Daniel Gardner, HfB

Todd Gill

Brent Jones

Anthony Notarfrancesco

Damon Savage

Peter T. Secker

Dave Sturgeon

Tony

Milton Keynes UK
Ingram Content Group UK Ltd.
UKHW040748020224
437154UK00001B/35